StringNet
教你使用英文同義字

李路得●著

英語辭彙不NG

本書介紹

線上語料庫是甚麼？

　　英語線上語料庫（corpus）是新興的英語學習工具。傳統字典的例句及教科書的文章大多是為教學而刻意寫作，常被質疑和英美人士實際使用的英文不盡相同，英語線上語料庫則是蒐集真實語料如英美國家的報章雜誌，將其中的單字或片語加以整理彙編，透過網路提供使用者在線上搜尋某一個單字或片語出現的所有句子。目前世界各種語言有許多已經建立其語料庫，英語最大的語料庫則是BNC（British National Corpus）（http://www.natcorp.ox.ac.uk/）語料庫，內容涵蓋英美國家的報章雜誌、學術論文、小說、廣播節目等真實語料，蒐集單字量超過一億。英語學習者可以藉由語料庫查詢單字及片語的上下文及其前後出現的搭配詞，以了解精準意義及用法，以此方式能夠學習真實世界的英語用法，特別在英文寫作的遣詞用字上有明顯裨益。

StringNet是甚麼？

　　在BNC語料庫中，英文單字與片語只有經過簡單初步的彙整，後來拜科技之賜，有一些學者把BNC的內容作進一步詳細的分類，能夠查詢更多資訊，本書採用的StringNet（http://www.lexchecker.org/index.php）是國立中央大學特聘研究講座David Wible教授主持創立的多功能英語線上語料庫查詢系統，內容以BNC（British National Corpus）語料庫為主，整理其中單字及片語，計算某個單字在語料庫出現的次數，若該單字有二種詞類，亦分別計算列出，以recruit為例，它可以當動詞和名詞，其動詞出現1934次，名詞出現871次；也分析某單字常常和那些搭配詞一起使用，提供片語字串，如recruit from和recruit new members等；還可依搭配詞的詞類分別檢索，並顯示搭配詞在語料庫中出現的次數從最多到最少，如recruit當動詞時後面出現的複數名詞有staff（28次）、people（21次）、members（13次）、student（9次）、workers（6次）、women（6次）等等，其中staff出現最多次，由此可知這二個字時常一起使用；除了顯示和常用搭配詞形成的字串以外，StringNet也提供包含某單字或片語的所有完整句子。

如果讀者有興趣多瞭解StringNet可參閱下列文章：

David Wible, Anne Li-er Liu, and Nai-Lung Tsao (2011) "A Browser-based Approach to Incidental Individualization of Vocabulary Learning," Journal of Computer-Assisted Language Learning.

David Wible and Nai-Lung Tsao (2011) "Towards a New Generation of Corpus-derived Lexical Resources for Language Learning," in F. Meunier (ed.) *A Taste of Corpora*. pp. 237-255, Amsterdam: John Benjamins.

Anne Li-Er Liu, David Wible and Nai-Lung Tsao (2011) "A Corpus-based Approach to Automatic Feedback for Leaners' Miscollocations," in A. Frankenberg-Garcia, L. Flowerdew, and G. Aston (eds.) *New Trends in Corpora and Langauge Learning*. pp. 107-120, London: Continuum.

如何使用本書？

由於StringNet的功能複雜，不易學習完整檢索方法，因此本書針對單字搭配詞的部分整理彙編，以俾讀者學習某一單字常用那些搭配詞，及這些搭配詞是否有共同特點（例如前面動詞recruit後面出現的受詞都是人類），並且把一組同義字合併彙整討論，以比較同義字之間的搭配詞有否差異。

本書的目的在於釐清容易混淆的英文同義字，編排時以英文單字的中文意義為考量，而非英文單字的拼法，因此本書內容之排序乃是按照中文注音符號，本冊收錄ㄅ到ㄈ，由於後續內容數量龐大，待日後陸續出版續集。為方便讀者查考，全書最後有英文單字索引，可以依照字母順序查考單字。本書包含92組同義字，每一組的內容分為四部分：

1.語料庫出現次數

藉著比較各同義字在語料庫出現的次數多寡顯示各單字的常用程度，例如：

StringNet語料庫出現次數

flatter	insinuate	fawn
482 (v.)	92 (v.)	42 (v.)

在此表示動詞flatter在StringNet中的出現次數是482次，動詞insinuate出現92次，動詞fawn出現42次。

2.常用句型和例句

幫助讀者明白每個單字可以出現的句子結構以及例句，建立上下語文情境的概念，例如不及物動詞（vi.）後面不能出現受詞，或某些動詞常用在被動語態，例如：

> **S + flatter + O（+ about/ on + N）**
> **S + be flattered + that 子句**
> **S + flatter oneself that 子句**

The employees were eager to **flatter** their boss at his birthday party.
His praise **flattered** her vanity, even though she didn't like him at all.
She **flattered herself that** she was the most attractive girl at the party.

3.常用搭配詞

若要探討的單字是及物動詞，則提供該動詞前面常用的主詞和後面常用的受詞；若是不及物動詞，則提供該前面常用的主詞和後面常用的介系詞或副詞；若是形容詞，則提供後面常用的名詞；但是不一定全部都提供，會斟酌個別單字的使用情形。以動詞swing為例，常用的主詞如下：

(det.) _n._ + swing

　　door, arms, legs, pendulum, hair, mood, wind, opinion, men, foot, tail, sign, boy, fish, gates, boat, hand.

　　在此(det.)表示可能出現限定詞a、the，所有格或量詞等，_n._ 表示下方所列的單字可出現在此位置，下方名詞從door到hand是依照在語料庫出現次數從多到少依序排列，也就是說door最常用作swing的主詞。在StringNet有完整句子，例如The front door swung open and Mrs Vigo came in, holding the child. (http://www.lexchecker.org/hyngram/hyngram_ex.php?hyngram_cjson=[30,%20287969]&meta_offset=105834492)

swing常用的受詞如下:

swing + (det.) _n._

　　leg, axe, balance, door, club, pendulum, gun, rod, bat, stick, gate, handle, scarf, hammer, basket, bag.

　　有的單字的搭配詞數量龐大，無法一一列出，因此筆者選擇較可能用在英文寫作的搭配詞，且名詞若單複數都有出現（如door和doors），則只列出次數較多者，形容詞若原型和比較級都出現，僅列出原型。

4.綜合整理

　　在此解釋同一組同義字個別單字的意義，並說明搭配詞的特性，以幫助讀者比較同義字之間意義與搭配詞的異同，在寫作時能選擇正確的單字及正確的搭配詞。

目 次

Unit 1 巴結、諂媚

StringNet語料庫出現次數

flatter	insinuate	fawn
482	92	42

flatter (vt.)

❖ 常用句型

> S + flatter + O（+ about/ on + N）
> S + be flattered（+ that 子句）
> S + flatter oneself that 子句

❖ 例句

The employees were eager to **flatter** their boss at his birthday party.

這些員工在上司的生日派對上熱切的巴結他們的上司。

His praise **flattered** her vanity, even though she didn't like him at all.

縱然她一點都不喜歡他，他的讚美仍然滿足她的虛榮心。

She **flattered herself that** she was the most attractive girl at the party.

她自以為是派對上最有吸引力的女孩。

She **was flattered** as well as frightened by his attention to her.

她對他的關注既受寵若驚又恐懼害怕。

❖ 常用搭配詞

(det.) _n._ + flatter

   scoreline, embarrassment, lords, Wilson（人名）, she, you.

flatter + (det.) _n._

   pride, him, them, host, father, ego, oneself.

insinuate (vt.)

❖ 常用句型

> **S + insinuate + oneself + into + N**

❖ 例句

Jim **insinuated himself into** his boss' trust.

Jim用心機漸漸取得他上司的信任。

She would **insinuate** herself at any price into the royal family.

她會不計代價用心機讓自己躋身皇室。

❖ 常用搭配詞

insinuate oneself into + (det.) _n._

family, mind, confidence.

fawn (vi.)

❖ 常用句型

> **S + fawn + on/ over + N**

❖ 例句

He won the position by **fawning over** the president's son.

他藉著巴結董事長的兒子得到這個職位。

Her friends **fawn over** her only because of her wealth, but she is unaware of this.

她的朋友因她的財富而巴結她，但是她渾然不知。

❖ 常用搭配詞

fawn over + (det.) <u>n.</u>

　him, beauty, government policy, doctor.

綜合整理

flatter	及物動詞，主詞可以是人或非人，受詞大多是人或與自我相關的名詞（e.g., ego, pride），主動及被動語態皆常用，表示人為刻意地巴結，使人高興。被動語態則表示某事情使主詞心中喜悅得意或受寵若驚。若受詞為反身代名詞則表示自我陶醉的想法。
insinuate	正式用字，指長時間以不真實的友善或誠意逐漸贏得信任或感情。另外也有表示給予負面暗示，或慢慢擠入一個狹窄的空間。
fawn	不及物動詞，表示為了得到好處而給予不真誠的善意或稱讚，後面常接over或on。另外也指小狗搖尾乞憐，名詞的意思是幼鹿而不是巴結的意思。

Unit 2 跛腳、瘸腿

StringNet語料庫出現次數

limp	cripple	lame
371 (v.), 186 (n.)	282 (v.), 119 (n.)	248

limp (vi. / n.)

❖ 常用句型

S + limp + adv.

S + V + with a limp

❖ 例句

The player **limped** off injured in the middle stages of the game.

這位運動員在比賽中場時因傷一跛一跛地退出。

He has a son who walks **with a limp**.

他有一個跛腳的兒子。

❖ 常用搭配詞

limp (v.) + _adv._

  back, off, away, along, down, home.

adj. + limp (n.)

  slight, pronounced, obvious.

cripple (vt. / n.)

❖ 常用句型

> **S + be crippled + prep. + N**

❖ 例句

Her father **was crippled** by gout several years ago.
她的父親幾年前因為痛風而跛腳。
Her boyfriend **was cripple**d in a car crash.
她的男友在一場車禍中腳跛了。
He is a **cripple** from his mother's womb.
他生來就跛腳。

❖ 常用搭配詞

a + _adj._ + cripple (n.)
　complete, partial, paralyzed, helpless.

be crippled by + (det.) _n._
　disease, TB, rheumatism, repeated foot injuries, osteoporosis, arthritis.

lame (adj.)

❖ 例句

He found that the boy was **lame** of his feet.

他發現這男孩的兩腳是跛的。

He saw a **lame** pigeon on his way home.

他在回家的路上看到一隻跛腳的鴿子。

One day his dog suddenly went **lame**.

他的狗有一天突然變跛腳。

❖ 常用搭配詞

lame + n.

　duck, dog, horse, pig, sheep, leg, people, man.

綜合整理

limp	可以表示因為受傷或僵硬而造成暫時的跛腳，或程度較輕的永久性跛足，當形容詞時只表示癱軟無力的而不是跛足。
cripple	多半表示永久性的跛足。cripple當名詞是比較老式的說法，現在被認為帶有輕蔑的意味，當動詞常以被動語態說明跛腳的原因（如crippled in a car crash.）。
lame	形容詞，多半表示永久性的跛足。the lame表示全體總稱，後面常接名詞，尤其是動物，注意lame duck是指失敗無用的人物或組織，或任期快結束且不會連任的政治人物。

Unit 3 擺動、搖擺、動搖

StringNet語料庫出現次數

swing	rock	sway	wiggle
3190	984	769	92

swing (vi. / vt.)

❖ 常用句型

S + swing + (O) + adv.
S + swing + (O) + prep. + N

❖ 例句

Suddenly the door **swung** shut behind them.

他們身後的門突然關上。

Michael **swung** his legs across the bike and hit the road.

Michael雙腿晃過腳踏車落地。

❖ 常用搭配詞

swing + one's + n.

legs, arms, head, feet, sword, body, hand, chair, microphone, umbrella, club, back, hips.

swing + (det.) _n._

leg, axe, balance, door, club, pendulum, gun, rod, bat, stick, gate, handle, scarf, hammer, basket, bag.

(det.) _n._ + swing

door, arms, legs, pendulum, hair, mood, wind, opinion, men, foot, tail, sign, boy, fish, gates, boat, hand.

rock (vi. / vt.)

❖ 常用句型

> **S + rock (+ O)**

❖ 例句

The mother **rocked** to and fro in grief, mourning over her dead son.
這位母親痛苦地身體前後搖晃，為她死去的兒子哀傷。
The mother sat **rocking** the baby in her arms to sleep.
這位母親坐著輕搖懷中的嬰孩入睡。

❖ 常用搭配詞

rock + (det.) _n._

boat, cradle, chair, child, bike, vessel.

(det.) _n._ + rock

boat, car, chair, vehicle, cradle.

sway (vi. / vt.)

❖ 常用句型

> S + sway + (O) + (adv.) + (prep. + N)

❖ 例句

Weeds **were swaying** gently in the breeze.
野草在微風中輕柔擺動。
The group started a write-in campaign in an attempt to **sway** legislators.
這團體發動連署活動，企圖動搖立法委員的想法。

❖ 常用搭配詞

(det.) _n._ + sway
　building, body, leaf, bridge, tower, lawn, opinion, crowd, people.
sway (vt.) + (det.) _n._
　vote, opinion, decision, jury, people, reader, legislator, belief.

wiggle (vi. / vt.)

❖ 常用句型

> S + wiggle (+O)

❖ 例句

They greased the ring and tried to **wiggle** it out of her finger.

他們在戒指上抹油，試著把戒指從她的手指扭動出來。

They are amazed when they watched Joe's ears **wiggling**.

他們看到Joe的耳朵擺動感到十分新奇。

❖ 常用搭配詞

wiggle + (det.) <u>n.</u>

　　fingers, feet, toes, hips, way, bottom.

綜合整理

swing	可當及物或不及物動詞，表示被懸掛在某支點上前後或從一端到另一端規律地搖擺，如盪鞦韆和門，揮劍或搖鈴則是以手做為支點。另外也指心情或意見動搖。
rock	可當及物或不及物動詞，指（使）前後溫和穩定地來回搖擺，注意rock the boat有找碴、搗亂的意思。另外也表示使震驚（例如The scandal rocked the entire neighborhood.）或震動使不穩定（例如The explosion rocked the ship and caused her to sink.）。
sway	多數當作不及物動詞使用，表示輕微地擺動，但是主詞通常是直立在地上。另外sway當及物動詞使用時表示動搖人心，也就是心態或意見的動搖。
wiggle	可當及物或不及物動詞，指以微小的動作從一邊到另一邊或上下來回擺動，和前三者不同的是它的動作很小，例如搖動腳指頭，或慢慢搖動以從一個地方挪移到另一個地方。

Unit 4 悲傷

StringNet語料庫出現次數

grief	sadness	sorrow
1293	762	655

grief (n.)

❖ 常用句型

> **S + bring somebody to grief**

❖ 例句

The sudden death of the new-born baby **brought the whole family to grief**.

這新生兒的猝死使這個家庭陷入悲痛。

They were stricken with **grief** and guilt after the car accident that killed their son.

他們為了兒子在車禍中喪生感到十分悲痛與自責。

❖ 常用搭配詞

<u>v.</u> + grief

overcome, express, cause, suffer, feel, bring, soothe, share, be stricken by, be overwhelmed by, be consumed by, be shattered by, be driven by.

sadness (n.)

❖ 常用句型

> **with + adj. + sadness**
> **a + n. + of sadness**

❖ 例句

It is **with great sadness** that our children will witness the extinction of polar bears.

我們的兒女即將目睹北極熊絕種，實在令人傷悲。

After enjoying the party, she felt some small twinge **of sadness** that it was all over.

在派對盡情享樂後，她在曲終人散時感到一絲悲傷。

❖ 常用搭配詞

a + _n._ + of sadness

  hint, twinge, lot, tinge, feeling, sense, touch, mixture, air.

with + _adj._ + sadness

  great, much, some, deep, post-coital, considerable, more, ostentatious, mingled, profound.

_v._ + sadness

  express, overcome, bring, hide, feel, cause.

sorrow (n.)

❖ 常用句型

> **to one's sorrow**
> **sorrow at something**
> **sorrow for somebody**

❖ 例句

In his book he expresses his **sorrow** at having to leave his country.
在他的書中他對於必須離開自己的國家感到傷心。

We share in the **sorrow of his family** and our thoughts are with them.
我們與他的家人同感悲傷，我們關心支持他們。

He felt so much **sorrow** from the death of his wife that he could no longer stay in their house.
他對妻子的過世悲傷不已，以至於無法繼續住在他們的房子。

❖ 常用搭配詞

<u>v.</u> + (det.) sorrow
  drown, ease, express, hide, feel, bring, have, encounter.

<u>n.</u> + of sorrow
  man, pang, period, sense, mood, lady, feeling.

綜合整理

grief	以表示悲傷的單字而言，程度最沉重的是grief，例如是因為所愛的人去世，因此常會以被動語態表示對受事者的鉅大影響（例如be stricken by, be overwhelmed by, be consumed by, be shattered by），後面介系詞常用over。
sadness	程度最輕，後面介系詞常用for。
sorrow	程度其次是sorrow，可以用在所愛的人去世或自己遭遇不好的事情，後面介系詞常用at或for。

Unit 5 保證、確保

StringNet語料庫出現次數

ensure	guarantee	assure	warrant	vouch
14032	3279	2916	1059 (n.), 761 (v.)	111

ensure (vt.)

❖ 常用句型

> **S + ensure + O**
> **S + ensure + that** 子句

❖ 例句

Sometimes a quantity threshold is necessary to **ensure** quality.

有時候需要控管數量以確保品質。

The government **ensures that** environmental impact assessment will be done prior to the development of the theme park.

政府保證在開發主題公園之前一定會進行環境影響評估。

❖ 常用搭配詞

(det.) _n._ + ensure

  system, process, program, hospital, government, company, right, act, measure, method, rule, condition, design, policy.

ensure + (det.) _n._

compliance, safety, consistency, success, security, peace, stability, compatibility, quality, accuracy, survival, fairness, equality, access.

guarantee (vt.)

❖ 常用句型

> S + guarantee + O
> S + guarantee somebody something
> S + guarantee + that 子句
> S + guarantee + O + (to be) + 補語
> S + guarantee + (O) + to Vroot

❖ 例句

Hardworking does not necessarily **guarantee** success.

辛勤工作不一定能保證成功。

Sex alone does not **guarantee** intimacy.

單靠性行為無法保證親密關係。

He is **guaranteed** a job at his teacher's studio.

他的老師保證在自己的工作室給他一份工作。

He **guaranteed** the young actor an audition for the leading role.

他給這個年輕演員保證讓他參加主角的試鏡。

He **guaranteed** her an interview.

他保證讓她參加面試。

❖ 常用搭配詞

(det.) _n._ + guarantee

I, we, you, right, constitution, law, government, system, treaty, contract, program, talent.

guarantee + (det.) _n._

success, right, freedom, safety, protection, security, access, independence, quality, precision, comfort, power, stability, immunity, growth, availability, intimacy, minimum wage, retirement benefits, profit, wealth.

assure (vt.)

❖ 常用句型

> **S + assure somebody + (of) +N**
> **S + assure somebody + that 子句**
> **S + assure somebody**

❖ 例句

The leather is genuine, I can **assure** you.

這是真皮，我保證。

The doctor **assured** the patient that he was not infected by the disease.

這醫生對這病人保證他沒有被傳染這個疾病。

Christine **assured** Kenneth that she would be waiting for him.

Christine對Kenneth保證她一定會等他。

❖ 常用搭配詞

(det.) <u>n.</u> + assure

sum, friend, minister, Maggie（人名）, life, time, quality, state, spirit, future, measures, staff, retirement, way, school, men, company, police, band, girl, Jesus, pains, king, center, headmaster, secretary, country.

assure + (det.) <u>n.</u>

tenancy, customer, residents, peace, readers, people, members, baker, Marian（人名）, standard, fans, management, parliament, journalists.

warrant (vt.)

❖ 常用句型

> **S + warrant + O**
> **S + warrant + (O) + that 子句**
> **S + warrant + O + (to be) + 補語**

❖ 例句

The author hereby **warrants** that the publisher is the owner of the copyright in the script.

作者謹此聲明此腳本的著作權屬於出版社。

The vendor will be asked to **warrant that** all documents and responses supplied are true and accurate.

賣方會被要求保證所有文件及提供的答覆都是真實且正確無誤的。

vouch (vi.)

❖ 常用句型

> **S + vouch for + O**

❖ 例句

He can **vouch for** me.

他可以替我擔保。

I can **vouch for** his intentions.

我可以擔保他的意圖（沒有惡意）。

He can **vouch for** the fact that this was not the case.

他可以擔保絕無此事。

❖ 常用搭配詞

vouch for + (det.) <u>n.</u>

   fact, result, truth, you, it, me, effectiveness.

綜合整理

ensure	表示確保某件事情會照預期發生，等於make sure，但主詞和受詞都不能是人，主詞時常是某個機構、方法、制度、或設備，而受詞則是欲達到的理想或狀態。
guarantee	含有承諾的意味，包括承諾給某人某樣東西，某樣好處，或自己為他做某事，所以也用在正式書面的承諾，如法律保證的權利、商品的保證期限與內容、以及擔保借貸的還款等等。guarantee和ensure有許多共同的主詞和受詞，表示保證達到某種理想或狀態，但是guarantee的主詞可以是人或事物，間接受詞是人，直接受詞則是事物，而ensure的主詞和受詞都不能是人，也很少有間接受詞，而且guarantee接的理想或狀態有可能是可遇不可求的，如財富（wealth）或利潤（profit），含有不確定因素。
assure	表示主詞向受詞擔保某件事情是真的或者一定會發生，以減輕其擔憂，主詞通常是人或可靠的事物，受詞通常是人。
warrant	表示保證某件事情的真實性，常用在正式官方的聲明，如保證版權和著作權等，後面常接that子句（例如The Author hereby warrants that the publisher is the owner of the copyright in the script.），也常用在對商品的保證。另外也更常表示值得或需要或證明為正當（例如What he has done warranted a punishment）。當名詞時表示逮捕狀，搜查令，委託書，或證書等。
vouch	指根據自己的經驗或知識而表示相信某事物是真的或好的，也可指為某人的品行做擔保，後面介系詞常用for，受詞可以是人或物。

Unit 6 報仇、報復

StringNet語料庫出現次數

revenge	retaliate	avenge
1023	226	138

revenge (n.)

❖ 常用句型

S + take/get/ have (one's) revenge on somebody
S + seek revenge for something

❖ 例句

The bombing was an act of **revenge for** earlier killings in the village.
這次轟炸是針對稍早村莊遭到殺戮而採取的報復行動。

The tennis player is **seeking revenge for** his defeat in the tournament last year.
這網球選手想為他去年在錦標賽落敗雪恥。

He and his wife wanted **revenge** on Rick for murdering both of their sons.
他和他的妻子想要找Rick報仇，因為他謀殺他們的二個兒子。

❖ 常用搭配詞

(det.) _n._ + take/have/get/gain revenge + prep.
　son, guy, earth, mother, team, king.

revenge for + (det.) <u>n.</u>

killing, raid, assassination, death, loss, murder, defeat, dispute, defeat, betrayal, voting, unjust treatment, murdered daughter, his people, Chris getting shot, making fun of him, what happened to her, the race four year earlier.

revenge (vi.)

❖ 常用句型

> **S + revenge oneself on somebody**

❖ 例句

One of the survivors of the Boston bombing sought to **revenge himself on** the attackers.

波士頓爆炸案的一名倖存者想找攻擊者報仇。

retaliate (vi.)

❖ 常用句型

> **S + retaliate by + Ving**
> **S + retaliate with/against + N**

❖ 例句

Japanese forces **retaliated with** heavy land-based aircraft attacks.

日本部隊以陸上攻擊機給予猛烈還擊。

Taiwan **retaliated by** refusing to attend WTO annual conference.

台灣以拒絕參加WTO年會做為報復。

❖ 常用搭配詞

(det.) _n._ + retaliate

British forces, government, the US, the Japanese, the Bulgarian army, the German Military, Iron Guard member, Muslim demonstrators, country.

avenge (vt.)

❖ 常用句型

S + avenge + O

❖ 例句

He swore to **avenge** his brother.

他發誓要為弟弟報仇。

Their deaths will **be avenged**.

一定會有人為他們的死報仇。

❖ 常用搭配詞

avenge + (det.) _n._

defeat, death, oneself, him, them, victim, murder, son, insult.

綜合整理

revenge	通常當名詞用在句型take/have/get/gain revenge + 介系詞,介系詞常用二種:on + 欲報仇的對象(仇人),或for + 欲報仇的事件(例如The bombing was an act of revenge for earlier killings in the village.),通常是私人恩怨,如謀殺、輕視,也可用在過去失敗的比賽經驗或對手(如The tennis player is seeking revenge for his defeat in the tournament last year.),所以前面的主詞也通常是個人或運動隊伍。revenge當動詞時為正式用字,很少用,常用句型是revenge oneself on(例如The Earth is revenging itself on humanity.)。
retaliate	是不及物動詞,也可以用在私人恩怨,但較常用在二個國家或組織之間的軍事報復行動,因此主詞時常是國家或軍隊名稱(例如Japanese forces retaliated with heavy land-based aircraft attacks.)。
avenge	是文學用字,及物動詞,和revenge一樣通常是指私人恩怨或過去失敗的比賽經驗,受詞可以是受害者或報仇的事件(例如He swore to avenge his brother.),revenge當及物動詞時的受詞也是受害者或報仇的事件(很少用)(例如The murdered baby must be revenged.),而take revenge on的受詞則是加害者,必須小心區分。

Unit 7 抱怨

StringNet語料庫出現次數

complaint	complain	mutter	moan	grumble	whine	bemoan
4422	4219	1912	770	436	272	119

complaint (n.)

❖ 常用句型

> **S + file/lodge/submit + a complaint**

❖ 例句

They lodged a formal **complaint** to the hospital about their ambulance service.

他們對醫院的救護車服務提出正式的抗議。

There have been numerous **complaints** against local government service.

已有很多人對地方政府的服務表示不滿意。

❖ 常用搭配詞

adj. + complaint

official, formal, few, main, often-repeated, British, general, quiet, endless, vitriolic, many, further, total, pained, individual, similar, well-known, specific, original, constant, querulous, self-righteous, genuine, common, intra-marital, populist, numerous, principal, frequent, bitter, usual, widespread, overall, major, innumerable, occasional, outstanding, several.

<u>v.</u> + complaint

receive, follow, investigate, have, make, get, hear, resolve, handle, lodge, answer, oversee, press, bring, produce, face, consider, determine, register, avoid, uphold, side.

complain (vi.)

❖ 常用句型

S + complain + that 子句
S + complain about/of something
S + complain to + somebody

❖ 例句

She got up at 11 a.m., still **complaining** of feeling tired.
她上午11點才起床，還在喊累。

The customer **complained to** the manager about the bad attitude of the clerk.
這顧客向經理抱怨店員的態度不佳。

❖ 常用搭配詞

complain about the + <u>n.</u> (of)

lack, way, noise, state, cost, quality, price, government, size, service, time, loss, security, waiting, difficulty, weather, heat.

complain + adv.

bitterly, loudly, mightily, vociferously, mildly, afterwards, repeatedly, publicly, effectively.

mutter (vi.)

❖ 常用句型

S + mutter about something

❖ 例句

The sick boy **muttered about** not being able to play outside with his friends.
這生病的男孩低聲抱怨不能和他的朋友到外面玩。

❖ 常用搭配詞

mutter about + N.

the unemployment, ingratitude, the ugly face, a neighborhood crime, storm for days, having to consult with his brother, his days in Paris.

mutter + adv.

darkly, thickly, hoarsely, ungraciously, quietly, angrily, fiercely, irritably, incoherently, softly, harshly, huskily, savagely, anxiously, grimly, gloomily, loudly, gruffly, aloud, abstractedly, rebelliously, acidly, silently, hopefully, crossly, impatiently, bitterly, defiantly, sourly.

moan (vi.)

❖ 常用句型

> **S + moan about something**
> **S + moan that +** 子句
> **S + moan at somebody**（英式英文，表示嘮叨）

❖ 例句

Julia **moaned** about her boyfriend not taking her out enough.

Julia哀嘆她的男友很少帶她出去。

His wife is always **moaning at** him.

他的妻子老愛對他發牢騷。

My husband **moaned that** I spent too much money.

我先生抱怨我花太多錢了。

❖ 常用搭配詞

moan + _adv._

　　softly, quietly, away, loudly, aloud, gently, hoarsely, helplessly.

moan about + _N_

　　the state of, declining standard, how fat she is, being in the group, the unemployment figures, the present, being picked up, the lack of.

moan at + _n._

　　each other, me, you, their team.

grumble (vi. / vt.)

❖ 常用句型

> **S + grumble about/at something or somebody**
> **S + grumble that + 子句**

❖ 例句

She **grumbled** about the hot weather all the way.

她一路上都在抱怨天氣熱。

❖ 常用搭配詞

grumble about the + _n._

   disruption, weight, decision, unavailability, hardship, treatment.

grumble at + (det.) _n._

   me, grandmother, stiffness, her, nature, change.

grumble + _adv._

   loudly, incessantly, aloud, quietly, privately.

whine (vi. / vt.)

❖ 常用句型

> **S + whine about something**

❖ 例句

The old man **whined about** his back pain.
這老先生因為背痛哀鳴。

❖ 常用搭配詞

whine about + (det.) _n._

   condition, cost, encroachment, memory, health.

whine + _adv._

   away, somewhere, softly, viciously, faintly, angrily.

bemoan (vt.)

❖ 常用句型

> **S + bemoan the 名詞 of something**
> **S + bemoan the fact that + 子句**

❖ 例句

The villager **bemoaned the lack of** medical resources.

村民悲嘆醫療資源的不足。

She **bemoaned the fact that** she had not been born one hundred years earlier.

她哀嘆自己不是在一百年前出生。

❖ 常用搭配詞

bemoan the n. (of)

　　fact, lack, absence, loss.

綜合整理

complaint	可數名詞和不可數名詞。指抱怨的內容，如顧客的抱怨信。
complain	對某個情況或錯誤的事情表達不滿意或不高興。
mutter	不及物動詞，低聲嘀咕表達抱怨或懷疑。另外也可以單純指嘀咕（如mutter under one's breath, mutter to oneself），此時可當及物或不及物動詞，語料庫的句子大多表示此意。
moan	非正式用字，表示以煩人的方式抱怨，例如沒有理由或不高興的聲音，moan about後面常接動名詞（Ving）表示某個狀態。另外也指呻吟。
grumble	及物動詞不及物動詞，一直以令人不悅的方式抱怨，grumble at後面的名詞比較常是人，grumble about後面的名詞則不能是人。另外也指低聲咕噥。和moan相似。
whine	以哀怨，煩人的聲音抱怨，和moan相似。另外也指狗等動物發哀鳴聲。
bemoan	正式用字，對某件事情表達失望。

Unit 8 暴徒、匪徒

StringNet語料庫出現次數

thug	gangster	bandit	mobster
703 (v.), 467 (n.)	237	189	40

thug (n.)

❖ 例句

A gang of young **thugs** killed a complete stranger on the street yesterday.

昨晚有一群年輕暴徒在街上殺了一個完全不認識的陌生人。

❖ 常用搭配詞

adj. + thug

   local, common, petty, tough, fascist, low-level, vicious, notorious, murderous, ruthless, Zionist, a gang of, a bunch of.

n. + thug

   street, company, subway, motorcycle, head.

thug + n.

   life, culture, world, violence, member, rap, lifestyle, leader, henchman.

gangster (n.)

❖ 例句

He looks like a **gangster**.
他看起來像幫派分子。
American Gangster is an Oscar-winning **gangster** movie.
*美國黑幫*是一部得過奧斯卡獎的黑幫電影。

❖ 常用搭配詞

(det.) _n._ + gangster
New York, Chicago, London, street, ghetto, Irish-American, movie, small-time, Latino.

gangster + _n._
movie, rap, disciple, boss, lifestyle, activity, role, violence.

adj. + gangster
local, American, dangerous, notorious, rival, Jewish, powerful, violent, ruthless, infamous, vile, mean, vicious.

bandit (n.)

❖ 例句

A British Telecom worker was badly hurt by **bandits** in Nigeria.
在奈及利亞有一名英國電信公司的工作人員被暴徒重傷。

❖ 常用搭配詞

n. + bandit

Liangshan, bandit, city, bay, mountain, forest, coast, urban, highway, border, road.

bandit + n.

leader, group, film, problem, mask, chieftains, force, raid, queen, lair, horde, movie, attack.

mobster (n.)

❖ 例句

Robert De Niro played a menacing **mobster** in the gangster movie.
勞勃狄尼洛在這部黑幫電影飾演一名兇惡的匪徒。

❖ 常用搭配詞

n. + mobster

Chicago, Boston, Brooklyn, opponent, New York, Italian-American, family.

adj. + mobster

American, Italian, ruthless, powerful, rival, fellow, local, small-time, vicious, retired, former, slick, notorious, legendary, ambitious.

mobster + n.

family, son, activity, boss.

綜合整理

thug	指暴力不法份子，尤其是年輕人。
gangster	暴力犯罪集團的一份子
bandit	是搶匪，尤其是攻擊旅人的搶匪組織，因此前面時常接野外地點名稱如沙漠、公路、或邊界等。
mobster	是犯罪組織的一份子，基本上相當於gangster，主要是美式英語。

這四個單字原形前面接的形容詞相似，如ruthless, powerful, rival, local, small-time, vicious, retired, former, slick, notorious, legendary等。

Unit 9 斑點、汙點

StringNet語料庫出現次數

spot	stain	smear	blot	blemish	smudge
5294	599	329	258	125	95

spot (n.)

❖ 例句

There is a **spot** of blood in his shirt.

他的襯衫上有一個血斑。

❖ 常用搭配詞

spot(s) on + (det.) _n._

  side, map, back, wall, horizon, top, surface, front, bench, body, world, sun.

adj. + spot

  white, black, dark, light.

stain (n.)

❖ 例句

If a politician marries a woman with a **stain** on her name, it might spoil his chances of success in life.
一位政客如果和一位名譽有汙點的女性結婚，恐怕會破壞他一生成功的機會。

❖ 常用搭配詞

stain on + (det.) _n._

　　fabric, paper, soul, company, plaster, clothes, sheet, redwood, honor, enamel, shirt, character, sofa, bedding, shroud, underwear, carpet, overall, mattress, ground, record, reputation.

adj. + stain

　　dark, red, guilty, biological, oily, indelible, lasting.

stain of + _n._

　　red paint, original sin, discharge, organic material, evil, bird dung, blood.

smear (n.)

❖ 例句

The candidate accused his rival of launching a **smear** campaign.
這位候選人控告他的對手抹黑他。
He went out with a **smear** of soap on his face.
他出門時臉上有一抹肥皂泡。

❖ 常用搭配詞

smear + on (det.) _n._

  skin, face, arm, clothing, character, page.

adj. + smear

  political, unwarranted, false.

smear of + _n._

  blood, silicone, paint, rubber, soap, grease, milk, sunlight, specimen,
  wax, oil, white powder, lipstick, soot.

blot (n.)

❖ 例句

The ugly building is a **blot** on the landscape.
這醜陋的建築物損壞了這裡的風景。

There are some ink **blots** on the document.
這文件上有一些墨漬。

❖ 常用搭配詞

blot on + (det.) _n._

  landscape, Britain, theory, history, reign, national character, face, human
  rights, reputation, copybook, administration, record, memory, civilization.

adj. + blot

  indelible, dark, shadowy, ugly, foul, moral, purplish, political.

blot(s) of + _n._

   dried blood, smoke, ink.

blemish (n.)

❖ 例句

Only God is without **blemish**.
只有上帝完全沒有罪污。
This brand of **blemish** balm is one of the best-selling products this year.
這牌子的遮瑕膏是今年暢銷的產品之一。

❖ 常用搭配詞

blemish on + (det.) _n._

   map, skin, record, face, administration, resume, victory, career, snow,
   forehead, landscape, saintly life, horizon.

adj. + blemish

   facial, spiritual, dark, historical, individual, red, immortal, artistic,
   orthographic.

blemish(es) of + _n._

   heresy, extramarital love.

smudge (n.)

❖ 例句

There was a **smudge** of chalk on the teacher's lapel.
老師的翻領上沾到一點粉筆。

The police found a thick **smudge** of blood on his car.
警方在他車上發現大量血漬。

❖ 常用搭配詞

smudge on + (det.) _n._
   record, girdle, manuscript, lens, face, picture, copies.

adj. + smudge
   green, dark, grey, faint, slight.

綜合整理

spot	有多重意義，用來表示斑點時，指的是圓形、顏色不同、平滑度不同（較粗造或較平滑）的斑點，特別指液體造成的污漬，也指人體或動物身上的斑點或胎記。較少抽象的意義，如個性或某種光榮記錄的汙點。
stain	表示不容易去除的汙漬，尤其是液體如咖啡、墨水等造成的，也特別用在人性的罪惡（例如stain of original sin, stain of evil, guilty stain）。
smear	是指黏的、油膩的、或骯髒的汙點，通常是被抹上或擦上的片狀（例如a smear of blood, a smear of paint, smear test抹片檢查），也可以指中傷，誹謗（例如smear campaign）。可指身體皮膚上的汙點。另外cervical smear testing 表示子宮頸抹片檢查。
blot	尤指墨漬、破壞景觀的建物、人格的汙點、或破壞好印象的事情。當動詞時表示吸乾或去除（例如blotting paper吸墨紙，facial blotting paper吸油面紙）。
blemish	強調破壞完美外表的汙點或傷疤。
smudge	等於smear，尤其指小範圍內的汙點。較少抽象的意義，如個性或某種光榮記錄的汙點。

Unit 10 頒布

StringNet語料庫出現次數

issue	proclaim	enact	promulgate
7804	1223	744	202

issue (vt.)

❖ 常用句型

S + issue + O
S + issue somebody with something
S + issue something to somebody

❖ 例句

The company **issued** its opinion against the price fixing.

這公司發表意見反對價格壟斷。

In November 1991, Yeltsin **issued** a decree banning the Communist Party throughout the RSFSR.

西元1991年11月,葉爾欽總統發布命令在俄羅斯蘇維埃聯邦社會主義共和國全境禁止共產黨。

❖ 常用搭配詞

issue + (det.) n.

instruction, order, share, statement, guideline, writ, bond, warning, warrant, decree, directive, proceeding, payment, bill, regulation, note, certificate, voucher, license, identifier, notice, information, leaflets, guarantee, invitation, summary, receipt, coinage, code, proclamation, advice, advertisement, rule, proposal, standard, paper, direction, letter, visas, demand, check, copies, banknote, figures, passport, permit, detail, law.

proclaim (vt.)

❖ 常用句型

> S + proclaim + O
> S + proclaim + that
> S + proclaim somebody something

❖ 例句

The prince was immediately **proclaimed** king after the king passed away.
在國王去世後，王子馬上被宣布為王。

Japan unilaterally **proclaimed** sovereignty over the whole island in 1845.
日本在1845年單方面宣稱擁有這島嶼的主權。

The Mongols accepted Russian aid and **proclaimed** their independence of Chinese rule in 1911.
蒙古接受蘇俄的幫助，在1911年宣布脫離中國獨立。

❖ 常用搭配詞

proclaim + (det.) n.

emperor, king, independence, innocence, love, law, belief, freedom, sovereignty, support, loyalty, neutrality.

enact (vt.)

❖ 常用句型

> **S + enact + O**

❖ 例句

Many Western states used to **enact** discriminatory laws against Chinese and Japanese immigrants.
許多西方國家過去曾對中國及日本移民實施歧視性的法律。

The Ministry of Education **enacted** education reforms focused on creating curricular standards and reducing class sizes.
教育部實施教育改革,重點在建立課程標準及縮減班級人數。

❖ 常用搭配詞

enact + (det.) n.

law, legislation, ordinance, policy, stature, regulation, bill, act, decree, ban, program, reform, tax, measure, amendment, vengeance, capital punishment.

promulgate (vt.)

❖ 常用句型

> **S + promulgate + O**

❖ 例句

The decrees were **promulgated** by the new king.

這些法令由新國王公布。

❖ 常用搭配詞

promulgate + (det.) _n._

law, regulation, rule, decree, constitution, idea, code, ordinance, doctrine, standard, order, standard, guideline.

綜合整理

issue	有多種意義，在此只討論二種：(1)公開發表聲明、命令、或是警告等；(2)政府等機構發行或核發文件等物給需要的人，如執照或許可。前面主詞可以是人或機構。
proclaim	是正式用語，表示公開聲明某重要事件的存在或真實性，常用來表達立場或價值觀（例如to proclaim oneself king自立為王，to proclaim gospel傳播福音），後面受詞可以是人或抽象名詞，它雖然和issue一樣後面可以接law，但很少如此用，而且多半用在to proclaim martial law，而沒有用在其他法令相關單字原形。
enact	是法律用語，表示將提案正式變成法律加以執行，後面受詞種類較多，如賦稅、死刑等。
promulgate	正式用語，使用量不多，意義涵蓋issue和proclaim，亦即正式發表或宣揚某種信念或想法。常見於宗教，尤其是天主教的教條或教義頒布，也可以接law和regulation等法令相關單字原形，受詞不可是人。

Unit 11 崩塌、倒下

StringNet語料庫出現次數

collapse	tumble	topple	crumple
2289	833	404	234

collapse (vi.)

❖ 常用句型

S + collapse (+ prep. + N)
to collapse and die
to collapse like a pack (house) of cards

❖ 例句

The bridge was hit by a bomb and collapsed like a pack of cards.
那座橋被炸彈擊中後像一疊紙牌般倒塌。

❖ 常用搭配詞

(det.) <u>n.</u> + collapse

　roof, wall, bridge, building, tent, temple, bed, undercarriage, floor, worker, stairs, gate, woman.

tumble (vi.)

❖ 常用句型

> S + tumble (+ adv.)
> S + tumble (+ prep. + N)
> to tumble and roll
> to tumble out/down/over/backwards/around

❖ 例句

Gold prices have **tumbled**.
黃金價格暴跌。

❖ 常用搭配詞

(det.) <u>n.</u> + tumble

　price, share, water, profit, world, waterfall, body, stone, children, rock, house, aircraft.

topple (vi. / vt.)

❖ 常用句型

> S + topple (+ adv.)
> S + topple (+ prep. + N)
> S + topple + O
> to topple into the sea/ pool/ mud
> to topple over/ backwards/ sideways/ forward/ off/ down

❖ 常用搭配詞

(det.) <u>n.</u> + topple

　　stones, horse, man, sideboard, chair, truck, head, man, glass, cabinet.

crumple (vi. / vt.)

❖ 常用句型

S + crumple (+ O)
S + crumple (+ prep. + N)

❖ 例句

He lost balance and **crumpled** to the ground.
他失去平衡摔到地上。

❖ 常用搭配詞

crumple + <u>prep. + N</u>

　　under the strain, into a ball, into the dirt, like the paper, against the tree,
　　like a house of cards.

crumple + (det.) <u>n.</u>

　　note, paper, leaf, map, telegram, envelop, sheet, page.

(det.) <u>n.</u> + be crumpled

　　he, car, land, clothes, brim, chair, napkin, sheet.

綜合整理

collapse	不及物動詞，指建築物或牆壁因本身結構損壞而倒塌，也可以指人突然昏倒。
tumble	不及物動詞，指快速、突然倒下或滾落，主詞可以是人（摔倒）、房屋等建築物、石頭等物品，也可以指物價突然大幅下跌，或水流、捲髮大量傾洩而下。
topple	及物或不及物動詞，可指一疊物品或人因不穩定而倒下，或使倒下，速度較慢，不及物動詞用法較多。當及物動詞時也表示推翻政府。
crumple	及物或不及物動詞，表示壓垮使縮小變形，如把紙張或衣服壓扁或壓皺，可形容抽象名詞表示摧毀（陰謀等）；當不及物動詞時也表示人的身體因失去控制而倒下。另外主詞是face時指臉部表情突然變失望。

Unit 12 鄙視、輕視

StringNet語料庫出現次數

contempt	despise	scorn	disdain	slight
1228	609	294 (v.), 216 (n.)	237 (n.), 42 (v.)	62 (n.), 35 (v.)

contempt (n.)

❖ 常用句型

> S + hold + O + in contempt
> contempt for + N
> in contempt of + N

❖ 例句

Theft is beneath **contempt**.

偷竊令人不齒。

He was found guilty **in contempt of** court.

他被判藐視法庭。

❖ 常用搭配詞

contempt for the + <u>n.</u>

subjects, Jews, way, views, law, wishes, emptiness, people, idea, feelings, job, potential, welfare.

<u>v.</u> + a contempt

have, show, develop, breed, conceive, demonstrate.

adj. + contempt

deep, utter, total, utmost, healthy, general, casual, bitter, public, apparent, equal, male.

despise (vt.)

❖ 常用句型

S + despise + O
S + despise + oneself + for N/ Ving

❖ 例句

He **despised himself for** having been in any doubt.
他對自己曾經有疑慮感到羞恥。

Abby Kelley Foster once said, "I rejoice to be identified with the **despised** people of color."
Abby Kelley Foster曾經說：「我以認同遭鄙視的有色人種為樂。」

❖ 常用搭配詞

despise + (det.) n.

melodrama, breed, irrationality, color, job, idea, boy, way, attitude, sentiment, discipline, community, people, practice, imperfection, the use of, sound, cult, movie, system, waste, removal, stupidity, relocation, authority, law, times, concept, thought, money, sign, school, woman, manner, film, precaution, fame, politician, hypocrisy, injustice, outsider, weakness, prophecies, foreigners, friendship, royalty, homosexuals, emotion, giggle.

scorn (vt.)

❖ 常用句型

> **S + scorn + O**

❖ 例句

He is an atheist and **scorns** the worship of God.
他是位無神論者，鄙視神明崇拜。

❖ 常用搭配詞

scorn + (det.) <u>n./ N</u>

theory, war, possibility, attraction, world, self-evaluation, woman, authority, relevance, claim, gift, suggestion, classes, triviality, establishment, proposal, experience, emotion, concern, number, superstition, Alice, attempt, make-up, religion, distraction, tax, voice, the use of, the idea of.

scorn (n.)

❖ 常用句型

> **S + feel scorn for + O**
> **S + pour scorn on + O**
> **S + V + with scorn**

❖ 例句

She refuses his gifts **with scorn**.
她帶著不屑的態度拒絕他的禮物。

They **poured scorn** on the "do nothing" government.
他們對無能的政府毫不留情地嘲笑奚落。

❖ 常用搭配詞

the + _n._ of scorn
   mixture, object, note, trace, deal, hint.

adj. + scorn
   withering, pouring, poured, angry, particular.

disdain (vt.)

❖ 常用句型

> S + disdain + O
> S + disdain + to Vroot

❖ 例句

They prefer simple life and **disdain** the use of technology.
他們寧願過著簡單的生活，鄙棄使用科技。

The ancient Chinese admired government officials and scholars and **disdained** merchants.
古代中國人尊敬政府官員和學者，卻鄙視商人。

❖ 常用搭配詞

disdain + (det.) n.

　assistance, admirer, artifice, vulgar exhibitionism, suburban embellishment, premature peace, autocue, half-baked friend, odious advance, invitation, childcare, the idea (of).

disdain + to Vroot

　reply, learn from him, use popular music, borrow money, consult a dictionary, discuss the matter, describe it, wear a left-hand glove.

disdain (n.)

❖ 常用句型

> **S + V (+O) with disdain**
> **one's disdain for + N**

❖ 例句

The little girl curled her lip **with disdain**.
這小女孩嘟嘴表示輕視。

There was an edge of **disdain** in his voice.
他的聲音中流露出輕蔑。

❖ 常用搭配詞

(det.) _n._ + of disdain

   look, expression, pose, air, mixture, glare, show, edge.

with + _adj._ + disdain

   such, haughty, mocking, cool, pinched, undisguised.

slight (vt.)

❖ 常用句型

> **S + feel slighted**
> **S + slight + O**

❖ 例句

He **felt slighted** because he was not the first one named by the host.

他感到被輕視，因為主人沒有第一個叫他的名字。

The boy **slighted** his black neighbors by calling them slaves.

這男孩輕視他的黑人鄰居，稱他們為黑奴。

❖ 常用搭配詞

slight + (det.) _n._

   desire, conservatives, people, you, motives, guest, place, god, chief, instrument.

slight (n.)

❖ 常用句型

> **a slight on + N**

❖ 例句

She took it as **a slight on** her job as a waitress.
她認為那是對她女服務生工作的輕視。

❖ 常用搭配詞

<u>adj.</u> + slight

  imagined, little, unintended, perceived.

綜合整理

contempt	表示輕視，覺得某人事物不重要，不值得尊敬。只能當作名詞。
scorn	強調批判的意味，視某人或事物為愚蠢、不合理、不理智、不值得接受或尊敬。pour scorn on表示強烈批判某人事物，對其嗤之以鼻。
disdain	是正式用語，類似中文的不屑，因為自視甚高而不願意做某事，或覺得某人事物不重要或不夠好而輕視他（它），有點高傲的含意，後面常接不定詞to-V。
despise	對某人或某事評價很低。也可以接反身代名詞表示對自己行為的不認同（例如to despise oneself for having been in any doubt, to despise oneself for one's weakness）。
slight	有冒犯、不敬的意思，只能用在人，常用句型有feel slighted。

Unit 13 避免

StringNet語料庫出現次數

avoid	avert	shun
11776	543	236

avoid (vt.)

❖ 常用句型

> **S + avoid + Ving/ N**

❖ 例句

Alice tried to **avoid** Sandy after their quarrel.

Alice和Sandy吵架後一直避著不和她見面。

The students are advised to **avoid using** unpublished material as a source of their thesis.

學生被指示在論文中盡量避免使用未出版的資料來源。

❖ 常用搭配詞

avoid + (det.) n.

accident, risk, confusion, problem, conflict, detection, attack, injury, ambiguity, damage, interference, obstacle, confrontation, persecution, combat, controversy, bankruptcy, exposure, loss, danger, enemy, destroyer.

avert (vt.)

❖ 常用句型

> **S + avert + O**
> **avert one's eyes/ gaze**

❖ 例句

They **averted their eyes** from the embarrassing spectacle.
他們把目光移開，避免看這尷尬的景象。

❖ 常用搭配詞

avert + (det.) _n._

    war, disaster, eye, crisis, threat, destruction, strike, danger, catastrophe, death, invasion, bankruptcy, violence.

shun (vt.)

❖ 常用句型

> **S + shun + O**

❖ 例句

Michael Jackson **shunned** publicity in his entire life.
麥克傑克森終其一生躲避公開露面。

❖ 常用搭配詞

shun + (det.) <u>n.</u>

　publicity, society, member, use, technology, the company of, contact.

綜合整理

avoid	意思最廣，涵蓋avert和shun，指避免不好的事情發生或刻意避開某人或某事物，受詞可以是人或抽象名詞。
avert	指避免不好的事情發生，受詞不可是人。
shun	則是指刻意避開某人或某事，受詞可以是人或抽象名詞。

Unit 14 標準

StringNet語料庫出現次數

standard	criterion
14993	5172

standard (n.)

❖ 例句

The car is of a good **standard**.
這車子規格很高。

Students have to reach a certain **standard** to obtain the scholarship.
學生必須達到某種標準才能獲得獎學金。

❖ 常用搭配詞

adj. + standard

　high, international, academic, gold, current, minimum, moral, professional, strict, ethical, American, official, general, legal.

v. + (det.) standard

　maintain, raise, assess, improve.

criterion (n.)

❖ 例句

The doctor told her that her son met the diagnostic **criteria** for autism.
這醫生告訴她說她的兒子符合自閉症的診斷標準。

The researcher needed a set of specific **criteria** for measuring language progress in this teaching treatment.

在這個教學處理中，研究者需要有一套標準來衡量語言的進步情形。

❖ 常用搭配詞

adj. + criterion

certain, specific, diagnostic, strict, objective, subjective, general, current, clear, basic, minimum, possible, clear, economic, technical, specified, formal, relevant.

v. + (det.) criterion

meet, review, devise.

綜合整理

standard	表示可以接受或是已經達到的水準，常用來形容某種已經達到的狀態（例如living standard生活水準）或大家所接納的標準（例如international standard國際標準，official standard官方標準），因此可以去評量（assess）、維持（maintain）、或提升（raise），意義的範圍大，在語料庫的出現頻率也很高。
criterion	用來判斷或做決定的標準，比較強調事先訂出來的標準，如醫學檢測或診斷的標準多用此字，前面常出現的動詞是meet/satisfy/fulfill等，常用的形容詞也是強調標準的精確及層級（例如specific和basic）。
此二字的共同搭配詞很多，在此不全列出，雖然意義上都表示標準，但有少許不同。	

Unit 15 邊界

StringNet語料庫出現次數

border	boundary	frontier	borderline
5042	4379	1343	187

border (n.)

❖ 例句

The mountain lies on the **border** between the two countries.

這座山位於這二個國家的交界處。

His experiment was on the **border** of a great breakthrough.

他的實驗快要有很大的突破。

❖ 常用搭配詞

border + _n._

guard, control, town, dispute, area, region, troops, county, post, crossing, police, district, country, security, line, regiment, issue, clash, trade, agreement, raid, plant, incident, patrol, zone, league, town, talk, demarcation, checkpoint, province, war, incident, fence, enforcement.

boundary (n.)

❖ 例句

They marked the **boundary** of their land with stones.

他們用石頭標示出他們土地的邊界。

the **boundary** between the normal and the abnormal
正常和不正常的邊界

❖ 常用搭配詞

adj. / n. + boundary

geographical, natural, national, city.

boundary + n.

layer, condition, commission, change, park, dispute, line, wall, fence, ambiguity, fault, marker, region, stone, ditch, treaty, talk.

frontier (n.)

❖ 例句

More troops have been deployed to secure the eastern **frontier** of the country.
更多的軍隊被部署在這個國家的東邊以保護他們的邊界。

The singer's latest album became the new **frontier** for soul music.
這名歌手的最新專輯將靈魂音樂帶入新的境界。

❖ 常用搭配詞

adj. + frontier

northern, military, new, French, German, final, efficient, imperial, present, wild, technological, national.

borderline (n. / adj.)

❖ 例句

The tumor in her breast turned out to be a **borderline** tumor.
在她乳房的腫瘤結果確定是交界性腫瘤。

The hill serves as natural **borderline** between the two villages.
這個山坡形成這二個村莊的天然界線。

❖ 常用搭配詞

borderline + <u>n.</u>

schizophrenic, autistic, cases, high cholesterol, obscene, patients.

綜合整理

border	純粹是指二個國家或區域之間的官方界線，包括此界線的鄰近地區，常用在與邊界事務相關的名詞，如border patrol agent, border protection and enforcement。
boundary	指天然的界限如河川和山脈；另外，boundary範圍較廣，可以大到國家，也可以小到私人土地的畫分界線，邊界糾紛可以說border dispute或boundary dispute。
frontier	是英式英文，除了可以用來表示二國的界限，也可以只單一國家的最邊緣地區，也因此frontier可以引申為在某個領域上已知事情的極限，如push back the frontier指的就是某個領域有了新的發現，也就是擴大它的極限使之進步；而frontier spirit則指的是早期美國開發西部的拓荒先鋒精神。
borderline	較常用來指二種情緒、狀態、或性質的分界。雖然可以當作形容詞，但是在StringNet語料庫中並未收錄。

Unit 16 邊緣

StringNet語料庫出現次數

edge	fringe	rim	periphery	brim
8901	1213	674	326	178

edge (n.)

❖ 例句

Their house is on **the edge of** the wood.

他們的房子在樹林的邊緣。

She sat on **the edge of** the kid's bed and read him a story.

她坐在孩子的床緣念故事給他聽。

❖ 常用搭配詞

the edge of + (det.) n.

forest, wood, bed, city, table, cliff, panel, park, bay, prairie, battle area, town, desert, airport, highway, shoulder, country, world, camp, group, crowd, ramp, road, valley, village, slope, desk, realm, night and day, Milk Way, society, page, wings, hill, tears, exhaustion, breakdown, bankruptcy, tragedy, acceptance, extinction, distortion, domination, panic, rebellion, tears, pauperism, penury, suicide.

fringe (n.)

❖ 例句

The senator was considered a maverick and remained on **the fringe of** the political mainstream.

這參議員被認為是異議分子，因而一直處在政治主流的邊緣。

❖ 常用搭配詞

the fringe of + (det.) _n._

district, land, area, park, town, south Asia, woodland, galaxy, boundary, selection, politics, movement, team, culture, society, acceptability, federation, community, political mainstream, entry level.

rim(n.)

❖ 例句

Red-**rimmed** eyes could be a symptom of blepharitis.

眼眶泛紅有可能是瞼緣炎的症狀。

He is wearing gold-**rimmed** glasses.

他戴金邊眼鏡。

❖ 常用搭配詞

the rim of + (det.) _n._

glass, plate, wheel, volcano, plateau, galaxy, crater, lake, disk, rock, Earth's crust, vase, snare, basin, wave, Great Canyon, valley, gorge, cup, sea, caldera, island, pit, drum, opening, coin, hole, disk, saucer, groove.

periphery (n.)

❖ 例句

Herbal medicine is on **the periphery of** medical practice.
中醫草藥是屬於醫療的外圍地帶。

❖ 常用搭配詞

the periphery of + (det.) _n._
　　crowd, city.

brim (n.)

❖ 例句

A waitress brought a tray of wine cups filled to the **brim**.
一位女服務生拿來一個托盤，上面放滿盛滿酒的酒杯。
The man adjusted the **brim** of his hat to shadow his face.
這名男子調整他的帽沿以遮住他的臉。

❖ 常用搭配詞

Vpp to the brim
　　filled, stuffed, packed, crammed.

the brim of (det.) _n._
　　pelvis, cup, straw, hat.

綜合整理

edge	有三種意義：(1)一個物件距離中心點最遠的部分，常指具體平面物體（如table, bed）、人群（如camp, group）、或空間（如square, area），片語the cutting/leading edge表示最前端、最先進（如the cutting/ leading edge of fashion/art）；(2)瀕臨某種情況（如tears）、狀態（如bankruptcy）、或時間點（如night and day），但這些名詞前面不加the；(3)刀鋒。
fringe	有三種意義：(1)窗簾或衣服邊緣裝飾用的流蘇；(2)在某個團體不被完全接納的邊緣份子；(3)一個物件距離中心點最遠的部分（＝edge）。
rim	是指圓形或環狀物的邊緣，如眼鏡的鏡框。edge和rim都可以加上東西南北等方向用來表示山脈的某一邊緣。
periphery	是正式用語，表示(1)某區域的邊緣；(2)非主流，不是最主要的人物或活動。
brim	容器的邊緣或帽沿。

Unit 17 辨認

StringNet語料庫出現次數

identify	recognize	discern
13102	5805	482

identify (vt.)

❖ 常用句型

> S + identify + O
> S + identify + N1 + as +N2
> S + be identified as N/ Ving

❖ 例句

The bodies of the victims have been **identified** by their family.
罹難者的遺體已經由家屬指認。

It was too dark to **identify** the faces of the men approaching him.
天色太暗，以至於他看不清這些朝他而來的男子的臉孔。

The child was **identified** as having delayed language.
這孩子被鑑定為語言遲緩。

Acid rain has been **identified** as the source of the disease that caused the death of the plants in the neighborhood.
酸雨被視為造成這一帶地區植物死亡的病因。

❖ 常用搭配詞

identify + (det.) n.

number, source, problem, people, face, type, name, gene, feature, information, location, character, area, object, member, body, cause, target, cite, element, need, pattern, author, language, property, resource, origin, factor, component, value, change.

recognize (vt.)

❖ 常用句型

> **S + recognize + O**

❖ 例句

He could hardly **recognize** her with her new hair style.

她換了新髮型後他幾乎認不出她來。

Most of us don't **recognize** the importance of health until we lose it.

我們大部分的人都是等失去健康後才明白它的重要。

❖ 常用搭配詞

recognize + (det.) n.

him, her, me, Gloria（人名），fact, point, problem, voice, value, symptom, potential.

discern (vt.)

❖ 常用句型

> **S + discern something**

❖ 例句

It requires wisdom to **discern** truth from lies.
分辨真相和謊言需要有智慧。

The hearing of a cat is very sensitive; it can **discern** sounds of its owner's footsteps from far way.
貓的聽覺很靈敏，從遠處就能聽出來主人的腳步聲。

❖ 常用搭配詞

discern + (det.) <u>n.</u>

difference, truth, pattern, object, fact, similarity, intent, meaning, detail, tendency.

綜合整理

identify	意指正確地指認某人是誰或某物是甚麼，例如在法庭指認嫌犯；也可指正確地找出或認出某物的性質，例如造成某種疾病的病菌。
recognize	是指依據過去所看過、聽過、或學習過的經驗而認出某人或某物。除了辨認以外，另外還有承認的意思，也就是認可某事物的價值或真實性。
discern	是正式用語，表示經過仔細思考後而注意到或瞭解到的事情，不能用在進行式。受詞通常是事物而非人。

Unit 18 辯論、爭論

StringNet語料庫出現次數

argument	debate	dispute
11968	8047	4304

argument (n.)

❖ 例句

They had a heated **argument** about who was responsible for the mistake.

他們激烈地爭辯誰該為這個錯誤負責。

He accepted the arrangement without **argument**.

他毫無異議地接受這個安排。

Islamist political **argument** usually rejects liberal freedoms.

伊斯蘭教的政治論點通常反對自由。

The scholar holds strong **arguments** against death penalty.

這名學者強烈反對死刑。

❖ 常用搭配詞

adj. + argument

main, heated, oral, strong, good, common, legal, logical, political, philosophical, valid, ontological, major, compelling, complex, counter, cosmological, economic, moral, convincing, rational, scientific, original, persuasive, much, theological, weak, skeptical, deductive, theoretical, practical.

n. + argument

closing, root, counter, opening, priori, doomsday.

debate (n.)

❖ 例句

The committee still couldn't reach an agreement after a lengthy **debate**.
在冗長的辯論後委員會仍然無法達成共識。

The two candidates will have a televised **debate** over the national economic policies.
這二位候選人將會針對國家經濟政策進行電視辯論。

❖ 常用搭配詞

adj. + debate

much, political, public, heated, considerable, ongoing, presidential, parliamentary, national, televised, intense, lively, philosophical, fierce, scientific, internal, long, open, academic, contentious, political, vigorous, theological, recent, extensive, constitutional, legislative.

n. + debate

policy, school, abortion, election, evolution, forum, candidate, budget, television.

dispute (n.)

❖ 例句

The territorial **dispute** between the two nations has lasted for centuries.
這二國的邊界糾紛延續了數個世紀。

She was currently engaged in a custody **dispute** over her son.
她目前在忙著打兒子監護權的官司。

❖ 常用搭配詞

adj. + dispute

territorial, internal, legal, ongoing, political, industrial, international, bitter, major, public, long, contractual, theological, domestic, heated, personal, financial, current, civil, jurisdictional, factional, acrimonious, religious, commercial, long-standing, local, diplomatic, unresolved, doctrinal, ideological.

n. + dispute

labor, contract, border, boundary, content, Wikipedia, copyright, succession, salary, conduct, property, accuracy, patent, custody, trademark, policy, priority, name, ownership, business.

綜合整理

argument	可以指(1)帶著怒氣的爭吵辯論；(2)就某件事情的對錯或真假提出的論點或理由。
debate	當動詞表示正式討論某一主題，提出不同看法以做最後決定或找到解決方法，當名詞時比較偏向辯論活動或現象，如電視辯論等。
dispute	表示爭論，反駁某件事情的真實性或正確性，可以用commercial, financial, domestic等字表示爭執的來源或範圍。

argument比較強調論點，所以可以用strong, compelling, convincing等字來形容論點的特質，但這些字就不會用在debate。Debate則比較強調雙方辯論的活動，可以用televised, presidential, open等字來形容活動的特質，但這些字就不會用在argument。

Unit 19 補償、報銷

StringNet語料庫出現次數

compensation	repayment	reimbursement
3188	1126	153

compensation (n.)

❖ 例句

The workers were given 20 days' pay as **compensation**.

這些工人得到20天的工資作為賠償。

One of the **compensations** of losing my job was having more time working out in the gym.

我失去工作的補償之一就是有更多時間上健身房。

❖ 常用搭配詞

adj. + compensation

monetary, financial, deferred, fair, total, partial, appropriate, reasonable, additional, minimal, inadequate, annual.

n. + compensation

worker, unemployment, injury, risk, accident, victim, cash, government, material, damage, disability.

v. + compensation

pay, claim, receive, seek, provide, demand, win, award, get, give, recover, make, offer, require, gain, limit, obtain, promise, want, order.

repayment (n.)

❖ 例句

They had little money left for recreation due to the monthly **repayment** of the loan.

他們每個月要償還貸款，所以只有很少錢用在娛樂上。

❖ 常用搭配詞

adj. + repayment

early, principal, monthly, annual, partial, immediate, symbolic, periodic, future, full, prompt, delayed, final, maximum.

n. + repayment

debt, loan, mortgage, interest, advance.

v. + (det.) repayment

meet, secure, trigger, afford, demand, make, agree, seek.

reimbursement (n.)

❖ 例句

The tuition **reimbursement** will take ten working days.

學費的報銷要花十個工作天。

❖ 常用搭配詞

<u>adj.</u> + reimbursement

full, federal, monetary, partial, small, maximum, third party, financial, dental.

<u>n.</u> + reimbursement

insurance, health, tuition, medicare, mileage, travel, expense, water, pension, airline, education, tax.

<u>v.</u> + reimbursement

receive, claim, seek.

綜合整理

compensation	有牽涉到身體傷害、個人損失、或財物的損壞。
repayment	表示還款，也就是償還之前借來的錢，如房屋貸款。
reimbursement	指報銷，亦即償還之前的花費，如出差回來後向公司報銷加油費等。

Unit 20 不滿意的

StringNet語料庫出現次數

dissatisfied	disgruntled	discontented
447	215	100

dissatisfied (adj.)

❖ 常用句型

> **S + be dissatisfied with something**

❖ 例句

He **is dissatisfied with** his son's performance in this contest.
他不滿意他兒子在這場比賽的表現。

❖ 常用搭配詞

dissatisfied with the + n.
  service, way, quality, job, decision, treatment, answer, school, work, amount, outcome.

dissatisfied with one's + n.
  life, work, relationship, position.

dissatisfied + n.
  parents, customers, clients, people, party.

disgruntled (adj.)

❖ 例句

The suspected arsonist can be a **disgruntled** ex-employee.
這縱火的嫌疑犯可能是心有怨懟的離職員工。

❖ 常用搭配詞

disgruntled + _n._

 members, fans, employees, shareholders, workers, woman, clients, drinkers, manner, face.

discontented (adj.)

❖ 常用句型

S + discontented with something.

❖ 例句

She is **discontented with** her work.
她不以目前的工作為滿足。

❖ 常用搭配詞

discontented + _n._

 workers, subjects.

discontented with + (det.) _n._

 work, outcome, lot, man, way.

綜合整理

dissatisfied	因為某事物不如預期的好而感到不滿意。後面接的名詞主要以人為主。
disgruntled	因為事情發展不合己意而惱怒或失望。後面接的名詞主要以人為主，也可以修飾態度（如disgruntled manner）。
discontented	對於現狀不滿意或不快樂，除了可能覺得周遭的環境不夠好，也可能指因為對自己有更高的期許而不滿意。後面接的名詞主要以人為主。

Unit 21 不活動的、閒置的

StringNet語料庫出現次數

latent	idle	unused	inactive	inert	dormant	immobile	quiescent
651	608	479	311	291	279	150	115

latent (adj.)

❖ 例句

There may be a **latent** period of 21 days before the symptoms appear.
在這些症狀出現之前可能會有21天的潛伏期。

❖ 常用搭配詞

latent + n.

inhibition, defect, content, demand, power, talent, stage, period, function, heat, syphilis, thoughts, inhibitor, hostility, energy, issue, learning, structure, knowledge, forms, potential, capacity, meanings, threat, variables, dangers, rivalry, anti-Americanism, anger, damage, phase.

idle (adj.)

❖ 常用句型

> **S + linking V + idle**

❖ 例句

The expensive equipment has been lying **idle** for years.
這些昂貴的儀器已經閒置了好多年。

❖ 常用搭配詞

<u>v.</u> + idle

lie, stand, remain, make, sit.

idle + <u>n.</u>

hands, curiosity, balances, man, time, chatter, gossip, threats, men, moment, thoughts, resources, speculation, boast, talk, speed, bastard, people, banter, dream, money, chit-chat, hours, fancies, minds, conversation, question, way, life, luxury, capacity.

unused (adj.)

❖ 例句

They decided to sell the **unused** piano before they moved overseas.
他們搬到海外之前決定把這台很久沒用的鋼琴賣掉。

❖ 常用搭配詞

v. + unused

  leave, remain, keep, grow, go.

unused + n.

  material, land, part, space, icing, equipment, allowance, fondant, portion, paper, tablets, condition, resources, food, records, permissions, side, energy, module, terms, hotel, farm, pages.

inert (adj.)

❖ 例句

The **inert** gases do not readily form chemical compounds.
這種惰性氣體不易形成化合物。

❖ 常用搭配詞

v. + inert

  lie, remain, become.

inert + n.

  gases, body, material, matrix, figure, waste, form, substance, matter, support, state, environment, compounds, solids, masses.

inactive (adj.)

❖ 例句

This new policy does not include citizens over 70 years old, who were considered economically **inactive**.

這項新政策不包括70歲以上的市民，因為他們被認為較少從事經濟活動。

❖ 常用搭配詞

 adv. + inactive

economically, relatively, sexually, totally, politically, previously, therefore, fairly, quite, largely, biologically.

 v. + inactive

remain, become.

inactive + n.

edges, crohn, enzyme, chromatin, state, form, disease, duty, caeruloplasmin, membership, account.

dormant (adj.)

❖ 例句

The volcano, which had lain **dormant** for 200 years, exploded last month.

這座火山休眠了200年後在上個月爆發了。

❖ 常用搭配詞

<u>v.</u> + dormant

  lie, remain, become, keep.

<u>adv.</u> + dormant

  largely, almost, currently, previously.

dormant + <u>n.</u>

  volcano, companies, season, company, eye, buds, files, support, area.

immobile (adj.)

❖ 例句

The dog remained **immobile** because of the effects of the sedative.
這隻狗因麻醉的效果仍然靜止不動。

❖ 常用搭配詞

<u>v.</u> + immobile

  remain, sit, stand, become, hold, lie.

immobile + <u>n.</u>

  property, labor.

quiescent (adj.)

❖ 例句

He moved to countryside to have a **quiescent** life.
他搬到鄉下為求寧靜的生活。

patients with **quiescent** disease
患有非活動性疾病的病人

temporarily **quiescent** earthquake zone
暫時靜止的地震帶

❖ 常用搭配詞

quiescent + _n._

   disease, state, cell, colitis, period, years, intervals.

_v._ + quiescent

   lay, remain.

綜合整理

latent	潛伏的，暫時不活動的（如latent period潛伏期），和dormant相似，語料庫未出現前面接不及物動詞的句型。
idle	不在工作中，不事生產。另外也有懶惰的意思。
unused	不在使用中或從沒被使用過。
inactive	表示不活動的，不活躍的，閒置的，停止參與以前常參加的活動。常用在生物醫學上，或者前面加副詞形容人在某方面不活躍。
inert	科技用字，表示惰性的，不能和其他物質產生化學變化的。另外也是文學用字指沒有力量行動，也有怠惰、遲緩、無生氣的意思。
dormant	表示暫停活動，休眠的，最常用來形容火山。
immobile	靜止不動。
quiescent	正式用字。沒有進展或沒有動作，尤其是暫時性的，常用在醫學上。

Unit 22 部、部分、部門

StringNet語料庫出現次數

section	division	sector
22809	11074	10949

section (n.)

❖ 例句

the commercial **section** of the British Embassy

英國大使館的商業部門

the reference **section** of a library

圖書館的參考部門

the woodwind **section** of an orchestra

交響樂的木管樂器部

sports **section** of the newspaper

報紙的運動版

❖ 常用搭配詞

section of + (det.) _n._

community, parliament, society, workforce, church, economy, party, population, nation, orchestra, profession, exhibition, higher education, industry, audience, budget, company, library, working class, vessel.

 n. + section

reference, rhythm, personnel, business, service, youth, control, development, sports, news, woodwind, finance, record, publication, string, brass, adult, policy, management, administration, food, woman, health, training, percussion.

 adj. + section

commercial, economic, corresponding, powerful, international, global, military, optical, advisory, existing, financial, industrial, photographic, musical.

division (n.)

❖ 例句

the criminal **division** of the court
法庭的刑事部

❖ 常用搭配詞

 n. + division

systems, league, cell, bench, services, family, products, premier, development, infantry, London, vehicle, north, operating, sales, research, technology, banking, engineering, operation, criminal, training, electronics, management, marketing, education, army, computer, traffic, communication, household, finance, agriculture, semiconductor, UK, car, health, leisure, publishing, consultancy, business, investigation, plastics, chemicals, statistics, second.

sector (n.)

❖ 例句

The primary **sector** of the economy includes the production of raw material and basic foods.

經濟的主要部分包括原物料和基本食物的生產。

❖ 常用搭配詞

sector of the + n.

economy, market, population, industry, community, labor, housing, profession, city, workforce, hospitality, health, regime, freight, business, country, company, catering.

adj. + sector

public, private, voluntary, financial, primary, informal, formal, industrial, corporate, commercial, retail, agriculture, secondary, maintained, southern, monetary, marketable, owner-occupied, social, urban, rural, tertiary, grant-aided, central, pharmaceutical, hidden, residential, British, military, civil, rented, economic, unionized, advanced, various, official, provincial, chemical, catholic.

n. + sector

service, manufacturing, business, state, banking, education, market, health, care, government, industry, university, transport, hospital, authority, energy, engineering, construction, oil, school, defence, enterprise, property, housing, electronics, export, insurance, technology, product, library, tourism, west, company, finance, goods, fisheries, dairy, food, retailing, gas, farming, mining, agency, monopoly, employment, welfare, household, currency, telecommunication, publishing.

綜合整理

section	較常用在具象實體的東西（如家具，建築物）、機構組織（如圖書館、公司）或地方（如道路的分段）的一部分，也用在交響樂團的樂器分部（如string section弦樂部）、人群（a large section of the audience）以及報紙的版面（sports section體育版）。
division	有許多意義，表示部門的時候通常指機構組織的分工單位（如services division），也可指軍事單位（如the tank division）或運動賽事的分組。
sector	尤其指商業、貿易等活動的部門（例如public sector公營部門，private sector私營或民營部門），但不一定是有形的部門，而是指一部分，可接of + 抽象名詞（例如the tertiary sector of the economy）。

Unit 23 爬

StringNet語料庫出現次數

climb	creep	crawl
5266	1459	1066

climb (vi. / vt.)

❖ 常用句型

S + climb + adv.
S + climb + prep. + N

❖ 例句

Zacchaeus **climbed** up into a sycamore tree in order to see Jesus.
撒該爬上一棵無花果樹為了要看耶穌。

She is a keen mountaineer who has **climbed** top 100 peaks of Taiwan.
她很熱中爬山，已經爬過台灣百岳。

❖ 常用搭配詞

climb + (det.) n.

　tree, wall, mountain, ladder, hill, stair, rope, tower, step, peak, cliff, rock,
　slope, fence, building, vine, harness, pole, stage, scaffolding.

creep (vi.)

❖ 常用句型

> **S + creep + adv.**
> **S + creep + prep. + N**

❖ 例句

Johann **crept** into the auditorium and sat in the last row.
Johann溜進演講廳坐在最後一排。

He woke up and found a spider **creeping** along his arm.
他醒過來時發現一隻蜘蛛沿著他的手臂爬行。

Religion **is creeping** into sex education in school.
宗教悄悄地進入學校的性教育。

❖ 常用搭配詞

(det.) _n._ + creep + prep. + (det.) _n._

error/ text, term/ culture, terminology/ encyclopedia, eponym/ language, he/ enemy encampment, idea/ film, a man/ office, development/ island, band/ national chart, influence/ band's sound, desert/ sea, bias/ decision, gloom/ one's life, night/ dawn, dog/ bull, religion/ environmental debate, ivy/ wall.

crawl (vi.)

❖ 常用句型

S + crawl + adv.
S + crawl + prep. + N

❖ 例句

Weak and bleeding from gunshot wounds, he **crawled** on his hands and knees outside for help.
他因槍傷又疲乏又出血，用手腳爬到外面求救。

The baby cried **crawling** to his mother.
這小嬰孩邊哭邊爬向媽媽。

We **crawled** into bed after finishing the report at 4 a.m.
到凌晨四點我們才爬上床睡覺。

❖ 常用搭配詞

(det.) _n._ + crawl

　　spider, man, search engine, larva, snake, creature, insect, ant, baby, monster, worm, bee, serpent, turtle, rat.

crawl + prep. + (det.) _n._

　　hand, floor, ground, wall, body, surface, tunnel, leg.

綜合整理

climb	不及物動詞，後面一定要接副詞或介系詞，指用手和腳在某物上面上下或橫向爬行。
creep	不及物動詞，後面一定要接副詞或介系詞，可指三種意義: (1)安靜而小心地移動，不引起注意；(2)昆蟲安靜而緩慢地移動，和crawl相同；(3)逐漸滲透影響。
crawl	不及物動詞，可指三種意義: (1)以手和膝蓋爬行，身體靠近地面；(2)昆蟲用腳前行；(3)因疲倦緩慢爬上床睡覺。

Unit 24 破碎、打破

StringNet語料庫出現次數

break	split	tear	burst	snap
18576	3090	2694	2340	2324

smash	shatter	crumble	disintegrate	rupture
1442	887	522	332	131

break (vi. / vt.)

❖ 常用句型

> **S + break**
> **S + break + O**

❖ 例句

They had to **break** the window to save the child.
他們必須打破窗戶為了救這個小孩。
Helen never **breaks** her promises.
Helen從來不食言。

❖ 常用搭配詞

break + the n.

law, silence, news, deadlock, surface, spell, chain, ice, mold, rule, hold, strike, club, record, fall, door, habit, world, agreement, glass, code, window, blockade, skyline, pattern, power, bounds, peace, lock.

split (vi. / vt.)

❖ 常用句型

> **S + split (something) into something**
> **S + split something in two/down the middle**
> **S + be split on/over/ something**

❖ 例句

The airplane crashed into a river and **split into** two parts.

這架飛機墜入河中並且裂成兩半。

His long face **split into** a welcoming smile.

他的長臉裂出歡迎的微笑。

The nation is deeply **split on** this issue of environmental conservation.

這個國家因為環保的議題而意見嚴重分歧。

❖ 常用搭配詞

split + _adv._

   up, off, apart, away, over, down, equally, evenly, out, fairly, open, neatly.

(det.) _n._ + split into

   face, orbitals, group, head.

(det.) _n._ + split up

   parents, couple, group, band, families, plan, fact.

(det.) <u>n.</u> + be split

vote, business, activities, band, sales, Europe, ministry, country, movement, opinion, family, head, party, data, responsibility, chain, children, group, office, chain, molecules, night, tree, people, society, network, costs, awards, remainder, trumps, revenue, parties, service, ministers, club, company, population, lip, forces, life, profits, time.

tear (vt.)

❖ 常用句型

S + tear something on something
S + tear something off
S + tear something out (of) something

❖ 例句

She **tore** her skirt on a nail on the wall when walking along the street.
她走在街道上時裙子被牆上的釘子鉤破了。

He **tore off** the page and hid it in his pocket.
他把那頁撕下來藏在口袋裡。

burst (vi. / vt.)

❖ 常用句型

> **S + burst**

❖ 例句

The flood was caused by a dam **bursting** after the unprecedented torrential rain.

這場前所未見的豪雨使得水壩潰堤因而造成淹水。

❖ 常用搭配詞

(det.) _n._ + burst

　bubbles, pipes, shell, tire.

snap (vi. / vt.)

❖ 常用句型

> **S + snap (something) off (something)**
> **S + snap (something) in two/in half**

❖ 例句

Suddenly the branch **snapped** and the boy fell from the tree.

突然間樹枝斷裂，這男孩從樹上掉下來。

❖ 常用搭配詞

(det.) n. + snap

rope, branches, harness.

smash (vi. / vt.)

❖ 常用句型

> **S + smash something down/in/up**

❖ 例句

The gangsters broke into his house and **smashed** things up.

這些幫派分子闖進他們家破壞東西。

The truck **smashed** into the shop; fortunately, no one was injured.

這輛卡車撞進這家店，幸好沒人受傷。

❖ 常用搭配詞

smash + (det.) n.

window, glass, car, place, ice, door, lock, radio, club, skull, record, ball, chair, plate, world, enemy, rock, back, windscreen, bottle, egg.

(det.) n. + smash into

car, bullet, motorbike, train, truck, debris.

shatter (vi. / vt.)

❖ 常用句型

> **S + shatter into + N**
> **S + shatter + O**

❖ 例句

His ego was completely **shattered**.
他的自尊心完全粉碎。

Most of the buildings in this area were **shattered** by artillery fire.
這個區域的建築物大多被大砲摧毀了。

The explosion **shattered** the windows of the restaurant.
這爆炸把餐廳的窗戶都震碎了。

❖ 常用搭配詞

(det.) <u>n.</u> + be shattered

　hopes, illusion, windows, dreams, evening, arm, silence, image, area, lives, peace.

shatter into + (det.) <u>n.</u>

　pieces, wastes, smithereens, fragments.

crumble (vi. / vt.)

❖ 常用句型

> **S + crumble (+ away) (+ prep. + N)**

❖ 例句

Some pillars of the old temple are beginning to **crumble away**.

這古寺廟的柱子有的已經開始破裂。

Be careful! The dried leaves **crumbled** easily.

小心！這些枯葉很容易碎掉。

The empire was **crumbling** after the civil war.

這個帝國在內戰後搖搖欲墜。

❖ 常用搭配詞

crumble into + _n._

  dust, ruins, disbelief, decay, sand.

(det.) _n._ + crumble

  apple, world, defenses, plaster, walls, cookie, path, marriage, regimes, bones, fruit, stocks, stone.

disintegrate (vi. / vt.)

❖ 常用句型

> **S + disintegrate (+ prep. + N)**

❖ 例句

This country is **disintegrating** into anarchy.
這國家正崩解成無政府狀態。

The old dam began to **disintegrate** a few years ago.
這個老水壩幾年前開始出現破裂。

❖ 常用搭配詞

(det.) n. + disintegrate
  system, party, army, car, control unity.

disintegrate + prep.
  in, into, under, on, at, before.

disintegrate into + (det.) n.
  anarchy, pieces, molecules, spheres, dust, chaos, puzzles, rags, fragments, splinters, whispering, factions, sobs.

rupture (vi. / vt.)

❖ 常用句型

> **S + rupture**
> **S + rupture + O**

❖ 例句

The liver of the dog **ruptured** when the car ran over it.

這隻狗被車子輾過造成肝臟爆裂。

The bomb explosion **ruptured** the fuel tanks and killed three of the crew.

這炸彈爆炸時造成油箱爆裂，三名水手因此喪命。

❖ 常用搭配詞

(det.) _n._ + rupture

fuel/oil tank, breast implant, pipeline, membrane, blood vessel, cell, cartridge case.

綜合整理

break	意義範圍較廣，指藉由擊打、彎曲、摔落而使物體破成二塊或數塊，受詞也可以是抽象名詞（如promise, law等），表示違反等意。
split	順著直線分開成二半，另外可以指均分為數等分，或意見或關係的分裂或破裂。
tear	用力撕裂（如布、紙張）。
burst	猛力爆開，以致於裡面的東西跑出來（如水管、氣球等）。
snap	啪地一聲折斷成二半（如樹枝），後面可加上不同副詞表示許多其他意義。
smash	用力打碎，猛砸。
shatter	破裂成許多塊，也指信念、希望等的破滅。
crumble	破裂成許多碎片（如枯葉），也指建築物或石像等因為年代久遠而逐漸解體粉碎（crumble away），以及王國、權力、或支持等的解體或削弱。
disintegrate	破裂成許多碎片且解體毀壞，或削弱、鬆脫而逐漸毀壞，也用來形容抽象名詞。
rupture	表示突然破裂或爆裂，例如血管或內臟等的爆裂。

Unit 25 破壞

StringNet語料庫出現次數

destroy	spoil	ruin
5974	1402	457

destroy (vt.)

❖ 常用句型

S + destroy + O

❖ 例句

The house was completely **destroyed** in the fire.

這房子在這場火災中被徹底摧毀。

He was accused of **destroying** evidence of the crime.

他被控湮滅罪證。

❖ 常用搭配詞

destroy + (det.) <u>n.</u>

enemy, world, city, building, planet, earth, life, house, monster, ship, evidence, property, power, cell, crop, civilization, order, humanity, universe, demon, structure, reputation, family, soul, missile, player, star, chance.

spoil (vt.)

❖ 常用句型

> **S + spoil + O**

❖ 例句

Spare the rod and **spoil** the child.

孩子不打不成器。

They were not informed of the party to avoid **spoiling** the surprise.

為了不要破懷驚喜，沒有人告訴他們有這場派對。

❖ 常用搭配詞

spoil + the n.

　ballot, fun, child, party, chance, surprise, plot, game, peace, tranquility, appetite.

spoil + one's n.

　fun, chances, holiday, day, evening, life, enjoyment, dinner, image, character, view, ballot, appetite, vote, story, child, film, plans, beauty, effect.

ruin (vt.)

❖ 常用句型

> **S + ruin + O**

❖ 例句

The sudden rain **ruined** the outdoor wedding.
突來的雨破壞了這場戶外的婚禮。

The wiretapping scandal **ruined** the reputation of the tabloid.
這個電話竊聽的醜聞讓這家八卦小報名譽掃地。

❖ 常用搭配詞

ruin + (det.) _n._

　　life, career, chances, plan, reputation, relationship, Wikipedia, world, health, family, economy, marriage, dinner, fun, day, business, wedding, appetite.

ruin + the _n._

　　appearance, soil, atmosphere, chances, visit, enjoyment, rest, things, day, hair.

ruin + one's _n._

　　life, health, career, reputation, summer, father, countryside, party.

綜合整理

destroy	指徹底破壞使之不堪使用，不能修復，或不再存在。受詞大多是具體名詞。
spoil	指的是破壞後該事物仍然存在，但已失去其美好的本質或吸引力，後面常接所有格 + 抽象名詞，表示毀壞某人的美好感受或時光；另外有寵壞、溺愛的意思。
ruin	和destroy相似，受詞時常是抽象名詞。受詞是人的時候表示使破產。

Unit 26 迫害

StringNet語料庫出現次數

oppression	persecution	persecute	oppress
721	432	211	202

oppression (n.)

❖ 例句

oppression and exploitation

壓迫與剝削

the **oppression** of women

婦女壓制

❖ 常用搭配詞

oppression + prep.

  of, in, to, by, as, at, for, through, on, against.

adj. + oppression

  political, gay, economic, linguistic, social.

oppression of + n.

  women, minorities, Romania, blacks, dissidents, mankind.

persecution (n.)

❖ 例句

the victim of **persecution**
迫害的受害者
religious **persecution**
宗教迫害

❖ 常用搭配詞

adj. + persecution

religious, political, Nazi, terrible, bizarre, Turkish, Catholic, systematic, severe, moral, rigorous, constant, illegal.

persecution of (the) + n.

Deng Xiaoping, God's people, Nero, church, Jews, protestants, Calvinists, nonconformists.

persecution by + (det.) n.

legal authorities, Christian Church, Catholic monarchs, man, reactionary government, Jingoes, government, federal authorities, Chinese troops, witches, money-makers, bureaucrats.

persecute (vt.)

❖ 常用句型

S + persecute + O

❖ 例句

be **persecuted** to annihilation
被迫害至殲滅
be **persecuted** under Elizabeth I
在伊莉莎白女王一世政權下被迫害

❖ 常用搭配詞

be persecuted + _prep._
   by, for, in, at.

oppress (vt.)

❖ 常用句型

S + oppress + O

❖ 例句

Australia aboriginals used to be **oppressed**.
澳洲的原住民過去遭到迫害。

❖ 常用搭配詞

be oppressed + _prep._

   by, in, for, within, through, with.

_n._ be oppressed

   women, blacks, workers, aboriginals, individuals.

綜合整理

oppress/oppression	表示不公的壓制，不給予相等的社會地位和權力，最常指婦女受到的不公平待遇。另外也指心情上感到壓抑沉重。
persecute/persecution	比oppress嚴重，常指因為宗教或政治等因素而長期迫害，甚至殺害。

Unit 27 派別

StringNet語料庫出現次數

faction	denomination	sect	clique
1426	377	358	113

faction (n.)

❖ 例句

The nation split into two rival **factions** as the result of the civil war.
內戰造成這國家分裂為敵對的二方。
The KMT divided into left- and right-wing **factions** in1926.
在1926年國民黨分裂為左派和右派。

❖ 常用搭配詞

adj. + faction

various, political, rival, different, major, small, conservative, radical, main, parliamentary, liberal, Palestinian, powerful, militant, right-wing, left-wing, military, dominant, Chinese, dissident, communist, terrorist, rebel, democratic.

denomination (n.)

❖ 例句

The Southern Baptist Convention is the largest evangelical **denomination** in the world.
南方浸信會是是全世界最大的福音教派。

Christians of different **denominations** joined together to pray on the global prayer day.

在全球禱告日不同教派的基督徒聚在一起禱告。

❖ 常用搭配詞

n. + denomination

Lutheran, church, Hindu, predecessor, orthodox, Catholic, mainstream, Christian, official, religion.

adj. + denomination

religious, different, various, small, Pentecostal, Presbyterian, major, Evangelical, reformed, conservative, Mormon.

sect (n.)

❖ 例句

The two main denominations of Islam are the Sunni and Shia **sects**.

回教的兩大教派是遜尼派和什葉派。

Soto is the largest Zen **sect** in Japan.

曹洞宗是日本最大的禪宗支派。

❖ 常用搭配詞

n. + sect

Buddhist, Hindu, Zen, Ismaili, religion, Beggar.

adj. + sect

religious, Christian, various, small, protestant, Jewish, heretical, Islamic, ancient, large, Muslim, radical, secret, fundamentalist.

clique (n.)

❖ 例句

A "ruling **clique**" is a group of people who jointly rule an oligarchic form of government.

所謂統治集團是指實施寡頭政治的群體。

The issues of high school **cliques** and bullying have received much attention recently and have been reported on TV news almost every day.

最近校園小團體及霸凌的議題受到高度關注，幾乎每天都出現在電視新聞。

❖ 常用搭配詞

<u>n.</u> + clique

　ruling, school, Shanghai, army, Brooklyn.

<u>adj.</u> + clique

　various, military, social, large, rival, popular.

綜合整理

faction	是指一個團體中的小團體，想法和其他成員不同且試圖使其想法被接納，也可表示團體中的內鬨。
denomination	同一宗教信仰之下的不同教派，彼此之間的信仰理念有些許不同，主要用在基督教。
sect	是比denomination小的宗教支派，主要用在佛教、印度教、或伊斯蘭教，而且有時候是指脫離原本宗教的小支派。
clique	是指一群自認為特別且封閉的小團體，不認同其他成員。

Unit 28 陪同

StringNet語料庫出現次數

accompany	escort
4703	763

accompany (vt.)

❖ 常用句型

> S + accompany + O
> S + be accompanied by + N

❖ 例句

He was **accompanied by** a girl, who proved to be a lesbian.
他身旁有一位女士，後來被證實是位女同性戀者。
The textbook is **accompanied by** two CDs.
這本教科書有二張CD。
Letters requiring a personal reply must be **accompanied by** a stamped self-addressed envelope.
若需回函請附回郵信封。

❖ 常用搭配詞

(det.) _n._ (should, will, must, etc.) be accompanied by + _n._
 photograph/ a brief description, quantitative explosion/ qualitative change, a bar code/ a long number, sheet/ explanatory memoir, the

woman/ a little girl, booklet/ explanatory leaflet, nomination/ signed declaration, military action/ congressional resolution.

escort (vt.)

❖ 常用句型

> S + escort + O (+prep. + N)
> S + be escorted + by + N

❖ 例句

The campus police **escorted** the guest speaker to a safer location.
校警護送這位外請講員到比較安全的地方。
The officer **escorted** me to the door.
那位警官送我到門口。
He met General Lee at the train station and **escorted** him around the city.
他在火車站迎接李將軍並且陪同他到市區各地。
A total of 61 aircraft **escorted** the ships and aircraft carrying President Franklin Roosevelt and Prime Minister Winston Churchill.
總共有61架飛機護送這些船隻與載送羅斯福總統和邱吉爾首相的飛機。

❖ 常用搭配詞

(det.) _n._ + escort + _n._

coastguard vessel/ shipments of, police/ staff, UN armed observer/ food convoys, staff/ patients, Peter's admirer/ him, cavalcade/ one's coffin, US war planes/ transport aircraft.

綜合整理

accompany	表示在某人身邊陪伴同行，或某樣東西附帶另外一樣東西（例如 The textbook is accompanied by two CDs.）。受詞可以是人或物。
escort	表示同行以保護（例如 The campus police escorted the guest speaker to a safer location.）或引路（例如 The officer escorted me to the door.），常用在軍事上的護航行動。受詞可以是人或物。

Unit 29 拋棄、放棄

StringNet語料庫出現次數

abandon	surrender	desert	relinquish
4329	1128	1034	492

renounce	waive	forgo	forsake
386	348	144	138

abandon (vt.)

❖ 常用句型

S + abandon + O

❖ 例句

The poor mother had to **abandon** her baby.

這位貧窮的母親不得不拋棄她的嬰孩。

He has **abandoned** his religious faith.

他丟棄了他的宗教信仰。

The burglar **abandoned** the attack after Judy screamed and bit him in the arm.

那名夜賊因為Judy尖叫並咬他的手臂而放棄攻擊。

They **abandoned** the hut at dawn and resumed their journey.

他們在黎明時離開了那間小屋，繼續他們的旅程。

❖ 常用搭配詞

abandon + (det.) _n._

concept, project, siege, city, plot, launch, garden, attempt, policy, (political) party, drive, vote, tax, dispute, idea, interventionism, standard, entrepreneur, rule, study, point, commitment, emphasis, principle, obsession, tyranny, monopoly, plan, scheme, system, career, meeting, search, process, effort, area, law, operation, ambition, conclusion, struggle, habit, sale, case, family, theory, march, issue, place, patient, person, movement, priesthood, competition, aim, pursuit, ride, task, chase, battlefield, science, property, job, protection, name, tournament, child, vehicle, doctrine, isolation, prosecution, publication, parish, practice, shelter, race, target, solution, round, lesson, attack, caravan, cause, focus, monarchy, nest, voyage, armor, stance, position, pretense, fight, car, method, assumption, hope, gun, symbol, conception, notion, market, field, conquest, religion, land, development, view, protest, expedition, ship, allegation, definition, diet, census, question, proposal, construction, expression, option, support, term, style, argument, custom, journey, congregation, effort, objective, scene, work, trip, warmth and safety, trial, privatization, disposal, arrangement, race, contest, production, implementation, calling, encouragement, approach.

surrender (vt.)

❖ 常用句型

> **S + surrender + O**

❖ 例句

The rebels refused to **surrender** their weapons.
這些叛軍拒絕棄械投降。

❖ 常用搭配詞

surrender + (det.) <u>n.</u>

lease, rest, initiative, lead, forest, territory, key, land, office, essence, site, seal, sanctity, embassy, copyright, film, power, title, patent, government, system, liberty, fight, safety, sovereignty, kingdom, belief, means, tactics, weapon, goods, profit.

desert (vt.)

❖ 常用句型

> **S + desert + O**
> **S + desert + O$_1$ + for O$_2$**

❖ 例句

The streets were **deserted** in the freezing night.
在這寒冷的夜晚街道上冷清空蕩。

She was **deserted** by her husband and went to stay with her sister.
她被先生拋棄，搬去和姊姊一起住。
Her husband **deserted** her for another woman.
她的丈夫移情別戀而拋棄她。

❖ 常用搭配詞

(det.) <u>n.</u> + be + deserted

　　children, clients, place, road, quay, area, hall, garden, landing, station, room, airport, building, city, square, woods and fields, newspaper.

(det.) <u>n.</u> + desert + <u>n.</u>（人）

　　the spiritual strength/ me, her innate vivacity/ her, the last of his energy/ him, all his cockiness/ him, his touch/ him, her vocabulary/ her.

relinquish (vt.)

❖ 常用句型

> **S + relinquish something (to somebody)**

❖ 例句

No movie star wants to **relinquish** the spotlight to let someone else be in the center of attention.
沒有一位電影演員甘願放棄聚光燈而讓別人成為注意的焦點。
Although the king was old, he refused to **relinquish** power to his heir.
雖然這位國王已經老邁，他拒絕交出權力給他的繼位者。
She was force to **relinquish** the custody of her only son to her ex-husband.
她被迫把她獨子的監護權讓給她的前夫。

❖ 常用搭配詞

relinquish + (det.) <u>n.</u>

grip, financial involvement, power, relationship, superiority, child, sovereignty, mandate, ownership, proprietorial claims, grip, post, one's hold, control, birthright, roles, activity, crown, money, autonomy, benefits, national identity, her, privilege, supremacy, connection, authority, neutrality, familiarity, land, position, territorial gains, helm, job, chairmanships.

renounce (vt.)

❖ 常用句型

> **S + renounce + O**

❖ 例句

Charles **renounced** his right to the throne.
Charles放棄他的繼位權。

❖ 常用搭配詞

renounce + (det.) + <u>n.</u>

use, world, throne, violence, claim, idea, devil, role, right, war, power, citizenship.

waive (vt.)

❖ 常用句型

> **S + waive + O**

❖ 例句

The victim's family **waived** their rights to an independent autopsy.
這名受害者的家人放棄自主解剖遺體的權利。

❖ 常用搭配詞

waive + (det.) <u>n.</u>
  exemption, clause, rule, need, charge, breach, right, requirement, privilege, provision, condition, restriction, sanction, death penalty, lien, obligation.

forgo (vt.)

❖ 常用句型

> **S + forgo + O**

❖ 例句

She had to **forgo** coffee because of her illness.
她不得不為了她的病放棄喝咖啡。

❖ 常用搭配詞

forgo + (det.) _n._

   chance, opportunity, festivity, right, dinner, luxury, service, interest, coffee, reward, benefit, pleasure, experience.

forsake (vt.)

❖ 常用句型

> **S + forsake + O**

❖ 例句

She will never **forsake** her children.

她決不會拋棄她的孩子。

He had to **forsake** the humanities and study science.

他不得不放棄人文學課科而改讀科學。

❖ 常用搭配詞

forsake + (det.) _n._

   throne, requirement, rugby, ale, dream, drama, job, turbo, screen, safety, pill, crisp, sympathy.

forsake + (det.) _n._

   throne, requirement, rugby, drama, job, safety, sympathy,

綜合整理

abandon	有四種意義：(1)拋棄對之有責任、義務、或同盟的人事物；(2)拋棄某種思維想法；(3)放棄某件已經進行的事情因為它有問題且無法持續；(4)離開某處，因為其不適合再久留。
surrender	表示被迫放棄某事物或某人。
desert	(1)不負責任地拋棄某人或某事物；(2)離開某個地方使之成為空無一人；(3)在需要的時候失去某種能力或特質，此時受詞是人（例如Her innate vivacity deserted her.）。
relinquish	正式用字。指放棄自己的權利、地位、和權力等,有不情願的意味,例如relinquish the custody of one's children是指因為爭取不到而讓出孩子的監護權。
renounce	公開聲明放棄自己的官職、頭銜、權利、信念、或行為。
waive	是指公開正式放棄權利、要求、控訴或規定等。
forgo	表示放棄擁有喜歡的事物或做喜歡的事情。
forsake	是正式用字，可以表示拋棄（=abandon），也可以表示放棄擁有喜歡的事物或做喜歡的事情（=forgo）。

另外yield在英式英文中也可以表示被迫放棄屬於自己的東西（例如The tyrant finally promised to yield power in a month.），和surrender相似。此字主要用來表示產生或讓步（yield to）的意思，在語料庫中雖然出現次數很高，但是很少表示放棄的用法。

Unit 30 噴出

StringNet語料庫出現次數

gush	belch	spurt	spout
174	140	116	106

gush (vi. / vt.)

❖ 常用句型

> S + gush + adv.
> S + gush + prep. + N
> S + gush + O

❖ 例句

There is a giant spring **gushing** from a cave in the limestone rock.

有大量泉水從那石灰岩石中的洞窟湧出來。

Light **gushed** into the dark space as the door was opened.

當門打開時，裡面的燈光瞬間照亮外面的黑暗。

❖ 常用搭配詞

(det.) n. + gush

　blood, tears, pyroclastic material, water, blood, wind, word, oil, bowel, spring, smoke.

gush + prep.

　from, into, through, over, to.

belch (vi. / vt.)

❖ 常用句型

> **S + belch + O**
> **S + belch + adv.**
> **S + belch + prep. + N**

❖ 例句

He could see the chimney of his house **belching** smoke.
他可以看到他家的煙囪冒出煙霧。

The dragon **belched** fire and smoke over the villagers.
那隻恐龍對著村民噴出火焰和煙霧。

❖ 常用搭配詞

belch (out) + n.

　　smoke, fire, fume, flame, mud, pollution, soot.

spurt (vi. / vt.)

❖ 常用句型

> **S + spurt + prep. + N**
> **S + spurt + O**

❖ 例句

Blood **spurted** from his neck.

血液從他的脖子噴出來。

A wisp of green fire suddenly **spurted** into existence in the haunted house.

那間鬼屋裡突然冒出一個綠色的小火光。

❖ 常用搭配詞

(det.) _n._ + spurt

  water, blood, milk, oil, fire, sound.

spurt + _prep._

  from, into, between, on, through, over, to, onto.

spout (vi. / vt.)

❖ 常用句型

> S + spout + prep. + N
> S + spout + adv.

❖ 例句

The volcano **spouted** lava shortly after the nearby area was evacuated.

這附近地區撤離後不久火山就冒出岩漿。

Flame **spouted** from the windows of the house on fire.

火焰從這棟失火的房子窗戶冒出來。

❖ 常用搭配詞

(det.) <u>n.</u> + spout

  blood, water, flame, gas, milk, fluid.

spout + <u>prep.</u>

  from, into.

綜合整理

gush	液體快速而大量的噴出。
belch	多半指氣體或火焰大量噴出，當不及物動詞時表示打嗝。
spurt	氣體或火焰快速而突然冒出，但是不見得是大量。
spout	意思和spurt相似，較少用，在非正式用語中表示滔滔不絕地說話。

Unit 31 胖的

StringNet語料庫出現次數

big	fat	plump	overweight	obese	chubby	corpulent
32610	2687	469	376	154	124	29

big (adj.)

❖ 例句

John was remembered as a **big** guy who often looked for fights in his hometown.

大家對John的記憶是他個子高大，經常在家鄉滋事打架。

The truck driver, who was very **big**, lifted the box with one hand.

那位個子高大的卡車司機用單手舉起那個箱子。

❖ 常用搭配詞

big + n.

  man, boy, guy.

fat (adj.)

❖ 例句

It is not polite to call people **fat**.

說別人胖是不禮貌的。

The world's **fattest** man is over 1000 pounds.

全世界最胖的男子體重超過一千磅。

❖ 常用搭配詞

fat + n.

man, controller, content, woman, people, intake, boy, chance, lot, lady, diet, bastard, cats, cells, face, body, legs, profits, slag, bloke, cow, tissue, cigar, hand, absorption, lesbians, consumption, stores, cottage, deposition, calories, cheese, substitute, malabsorption, yoghurt, distribution, cheque, book, milk, lips, bacon, baby, meat, parasites.

plump (adj.)

❖ 例句

The actress' slightly **plump** figure attracts attention and fans.
這名女演員稍微豐腴的身材吸引不少注意和粉絲。

The portrait shows a girl with **plump** face in a luxurious gown.
這個肖像是一位臉龐圓潤，穿著華麗長袍的女孩子。

❖ 常用搭配詞

plump + n.

bird, pigeon, body, face, figure, neck, boy, chicken, female, sister, girl, appearance.

overweight (adj.)

❖ 例句

People who are **overweight** are more likely to have heart attacks.
體重過重的人容易有心臟病發作。

Many people feel they are **overweight** even though they are not.
許多人覺得自己體重過重，即使事實不然。

❖ 常用搭配詞

overweight + n.

people, person, host, individual, animal, friends, man, lady, thigh, kid, mother, baby, smoker, children.

obese (adj.)

❖ 例句

His job is help seriously **obese** people lose weight.
他的工作是幫助嚴重過胖的人減重。

Obese women tend to have negative self-image.
過胖的女性容易有負面的自我形象。

❖ 常用搭配詞

obese + n.

people, patient, man, individual, woman, person, appearance, wrestler, baby, mother, boy.

chubby (adj.)

❖ 例句

The stereotype of Santa Claus is a short, **chubby** man with a round red face.
聖誕老公公的傳統形象是身材矮胖，臉色圓潤。

When he was a little boy, his aunts liked to pinch his **chubby** cheeks every time they visited his home.
他小時候他的阿姨們每次來他家拜訪時都喜歡捏他圓胖的臉頰。

❖ 常用搭配詞

chubby + n.

  face, hand, finger, cheek, baby, kid, body, limp, sister, fist, leg, bunny, figure.

corpulent (adj.)

❖ 例句

He died of apoplexy, which appeared plausible as he was a **corpulent** man.
他死於中風，看來合理，因為他身材肥胖。

❖ 常用搭配詞

corpulent + n.

  man, wizard, body, pal.

綜合整理

big	是對於高大、強壯、或肥胖的身軀比較禮貌的說法，常用來形容男性。
fat	是直接而不禮貌的說法，最好只用來形容自己。另外也指巨額的或寬厚的。
plump	是好看的胖，類似中文的豐滿，常用來形容女性。
overweight	是對於過胖或變胖禮貌的說法。
obese	是醫學名詞，常被醫生用來表示對健康有害的肥胖。
chubby	是非正式用語，常用來形容小孩或身體某一部位的圓胖，也常和short一起使用表示矮胖。
corpulent	是fat的正式用語，不常使用。

Unit 32 批評

StringNet語料庫出現次數

judge	comment	criticize
4667	4430	1687

judge (vi. / vt.)

❖ 常用句型

S + judge + N + by something
S + judge + N (to be) something
S + judge + that/whether/ how /（疑問詞）＋ 子句

❖ 例句

The contestants will be **judged** on their performance and costumes.
參賽者會依他們的表現和服裝被評分。

The Bible says, "For as you have been **judging**, so you will be judged."
聖經上說：「因為你們怎樣論斷人，也必怎樣被論斷。」

❖ 常用搭配詞

judge by/on + (det.) _n._

works, behavior, ability, merit, performance, success, form, usefulness, standard, convention, predictive power, end-result, contribution, winning, competence, willingness, effect, appearance, career, effectiveness, predicament.

comment (vi. / vt.)

❖ 常用句型

> **S + comment + on/upon + N**
> **S + comment + that 子句**

❖ 例句

People like to **comment on** the celebrity's private life.
人們喜歡對名人的私生活品頭論足。
The mayor refused to **comment on** his divorce.
這市長拒絕對他的離婚發表評論。

❖ 常用搭配詞

comment on + (det.) <u>n.</u>
   award, issue, leak, content, rumor, letter, possibility, claim, visit, meeting,
   report, allegation, decision, case, talk, plan, contract.

criticize (vi. / vt.)

❖ 常用句型

> **S + criticize + O + for (doing) something**
> **S + criticize + O + as something**

❖ 例句

The philosopher's new book is **criticized as** lacking rigor and analytic content.
這位哲學家的新書被批評內容分析鬆散不夠嚴謹。

The candidate **criticized** her opponent for his ungrounded remarks.
這候選人批評她的對手言論沒有根據。

❖ 常用搭配詞

(det.) _n._ + be criticized (for)

  convention, theory, proposal, Board, criterion, concept, notion, project, administrator, policy, Japan, leadership, plan, company, system, failure, move, allocation, reduction, government, approach, speech.

criticize + (det.) _n._

  government, policy, president, decision, work, action, use, game, people, book, idea, theory, opponent, film, leadership, method, administration.

綜合整理

judge	是指經過深思熟慮與全盤考量之後對一件事情或一個人的性質作出判斷,例如表演活動的裁判或對一個人品性的論斷。
comment	指的是針對某件事情或某人表達意見或發表評論,有說長道短的含意。
criticize	有批評、挑錯、指責等的負面意思,常用在文學、藝術作品的批判。

Unit 33 疲倦的

StringNet語料庫出現次數

tired	weary	exhausted	drained
3682	656	524	153

drowsy	listless	flagging	fatigued
146	72	53	38

tired (adj.)

❖ 例句

Nick is **tired** of the constant battle between his parents and wants to move out.

Nick 厭煩經常和他的父母爭執，想搬出來住。

The **tired** sailor finally went back to his hometown.

這名疲倦的水手終於回到他的家鄉。

❖ 常用搭配詞

tired + n.

　mind, soul, eye, man, sailor.

weary (adj.)

❖ 例句

I sat down to rest my **weary** legs.
我雙腿疲累，便坐下休息。
The farmer looked old and **weary**.
這農夫看起來又老又疲憊。

weary + n.

  smile, muscle, patience, walker, constituency, limb, shopper, reluctance, troop, body, visitor, feeling, salute, head, lids, people, runner, arm, immigrant, feet, voice, sigh, anger, traveler.

exhausted (adj.)

❖ 常用句型

S + be exhausted (+ from/ by + N)

❖ 例句

She was too **exhausted** to take a shower and fell asleep on the sofa.
她累到沒力氣洗澡，在沙發上睡著了。
He hauled his **exhausted** body back to his room.
他拖著精疲力盡的身體回到他的房間。

He is **exhausted** from the election campaign.
他為了選舉活動而精疲力盡。

❖ 常用搭配詞

exhausted + n.

escapee, neck, emigrant, delegate, silence, woman, refugee, colleague,
rescuer, sleep, girl, exultation, body, figure, captain, mother, crew, parent.

drained (adj.)

❖ 例句

I feel **drained**, both physically and mentally.
我覺得我的身體和心靈都被榨乾了。

❖ 常用搭配詞

v. + drained

feel, look, seem.

drained and + adj.

empty, weary, tired, exhausted, despondent.

drowsy (adj.)

❖ 例句

The drug made me so **drowsy** that I couldn't drive to work.
這藥令我想睡，因此不能開車去工作。

常用搭配詞

v. + drowsy

　　feel, become, get, appear.

drowsy and + adj.

　　slow, numb, tired.

listless (adj.)

❖ 例句

He went home feeling tired and **listless**.
他又倦怠又無精打采地回家。

❖ 常用搭配詞

listless + n.

　　race, voice, fashion, attitude.

flagging (adj.)

❖ 例句

The most important thing for the new government is to boost the **flagging** economy.
新政府的最重要的事情是提振衰弱的經濟。

❖ 常用搭配詞

flagging + n.

　　economy, fortunes, career, intifada, spirits, popularity, energy.

fatigued (adj.)

❖ 例句

During the period of losing weight, she became easily **fatigued**.
在減重的過程，她變得很容易疲勞。

綜合整理

tired	表示想休息或睡覺的感覺，後面通常不接名詞，若接名詞則通常表示長期或心靈的疲憊，如tired minds，時常出現在too…to句型。
exhausted	表示極度疲倦，時常出現在too…to句型。
weary	強調因勞動後的疲憊感，後面常接名詞，前面常接所有格，如my weary legs。be weary of和be tired of都表示厭倦。
drained	筋疲力盡。當動詞表示排水，流出，或耗盡。
drowsy	累得幾乎要睡著，也指令人想睡的（如a drowsy afternoon）。
listless	感覺無精打采、疲倦、或懶洋洋。
flagging	疲倦或無力，也表示經濟等疲軟。不用在形容人，而是形容經濟或人的精神士氣等。
fatigued	極端疲倦，等於exhausted。在語料庫出現次數少，故不提供搭配詞。

Unit 34 漂泊、流浪

StringNet語料庫出現次數

wander	drift	roam	stray
2337	1919	526	490

wander (vi. / vt.)

❖ 常用句型

> S + wander + perp. + N
> S + wander + O

❖ 例句

We **wandered** round the gallery while waiting for our flight.
在等我們的班機時，我們在長廊（畫廊）閒晃。
He **wandered** the city looking for a job.
他在這城市中到處找工作。

❖ 常用搭配詞

wander round + (det.) <u>n.</u>
   street, house, church, library, gallery, village, hill, area, camp, town.

wander through + (det.) <u>n.</u>
   wilderness, market, highland, Wikipedia, city, hall, mist, area.

(det.) n. + wander

people, child, mind.

wander + (det.) n.

streets, earth, hills, world, corridors, countryside, lanes.

drift (vi.)

❖ 常用句型

S + drift (+ adv.) + prep. + N

❖ 例句

The sound of the music **drifted** down from the monastery on the hill.

音樂聲從修道院飄揚到山下。

She **drifted** into sleep while he was reading the bed story.

當他在唸床邊故事時,她逐漸陷入夢鄉。

❖ 常用搭配詞

(det.) n. + drift away

dream, talk, mind, thoughts, people, crowd, blue, purple, balloon, gaze, glance.

(det.) n. + drift down

rate, number, snow, flake, music, smell, eyes, hand, boat.

drift into + n.

sleep, despair, war, darkness, intimacy, delinquency, crime, stagnation, complacency.

roam (vi. / vt.)

❖ 常用句型

> S + roam + perp. + N
> S + roam + O

❖ 例句

On the day of the Water Festival, people **roam** the streets with bowls of water and drench each other and passersby.

潑水節當天，人們拿著碗裝的水在街上遊走，互相潑水，對過路人也不例外。

Dinosaurs **roamed** the earth 200 million years ago.

在二億年前恐龍在地球出沒。

His eyes **roamed** over the chattering women, assessing them.

他的目光在那些聊天的女孩身上遊走打量著她們。

❖ 常用搭配詞

(det.) _n._ + roam

monster, creature, animal, herd, dinosaur, band, spirit, people.

roam + (det.) _n._

streets, world, countryside, country, desert, earth, forests, room, area, fields, globe, neighborhood, city, hills, skies, corridors, park, land, ground.

stray (vi.)

❖ 常用句型

> **S + stray + prep. + N**

❖ 例句

The lions will ruthlessly attack other males that **stray** into their territories.
這些獅子會毫不留情攻擊其他闖入牠們地盤的流浪公獅。

In his office his mind often **strayed** from what he was doing worrying about his dying wife.
他在辦公室做事時經常會恍神，因為掛念他快過世的妻子。

❖ 常用搭配詞

(det.) _n._ + stray
eyes, thoughts, dog, cattle.

stray from + (det.) _n._
point, agreement, path, herd, group, line, debate.

stray into + (det.) _n._
forbidden part, territory, restricted area, foreign country, situation.

綜合整理

wander	指無目的也無方向地緩慢四處走動,尤其是在室內建築(如house, church)。另外也指心思意念因為疲倦或無趣而飄移不專心。
drift	指在水中或空中飄移,強調位置或狀態的轉變。
roam	無目的也無方向地在廣大地區行走,尤其是長時間,主詞常是動物。
stray	離開平常或正常的路。另也指眼神無目的地游移。

Unit 35 偏見

StringNet語料庫出現次數

prejudice	bias	partiality
1520	1339	69

prejudice (n.)

❖ 例句

In his autobiography he talked about his experience with racial **prejudice** while working in Florida.

在他的自傳中他談到在佛州工作時遭受的種族偏見。

❖ 常用搭配詞

adj. + prejudice

racial, extreme, religious, personal, popular, anti-Semitic, common, political, cultural, ethnic.

prejudice and _n._

fear, oppression, hatred, unfairness, ignorance, resistance, stereotyping, suspicion, hysteria.

bias (n.)

❖ 例句

NPOV (Neutral Point Of View) is an official Wikipedia policy which requires that articles should represent all views fairly and without **bias**.
觀點中立是維基百科的官方政策，要求所有文章的觀點必須公平無偏見。

❖ 常用搭配詞

adj. + bias

systemic, liberal, cognitive, cultural, political, personal, systematic, racial, left-wing, alleged, ideological, inherent, unconscious, blatant, inbuilt, significant, pronounced, heavy, instinct, existing.

partiality (n.)

❖ 例句

Their victory was considered a sign of God's **partiality** for their country.
他們的勝利被視為是上帝特別恩待他們國家的象徵。
Parental **partiality** often leads to jealousy among siblings.
父母的偏心經常導致手足間的爭風吃醋。

❖ 常用搭配詞

adj. + partiality

empathetic, distinct, critical, alleged, one-sided, disciplinary, royal, marked.

綜合整理

prejudice	指偏見，是非理性、先入為主的主觀判斷，通常伴隨負面的情緒，因此常與負面名詞一起出現（如hatred, oppression, ignorance等）。
bias	指的是理性上的錯誤判斷，往往是prejudice造成的結果，常用在法令，政治方面。
partiality	是指個人的偏愛。
bias前面最常接形容詞，prejudice次之，partiality極少。	

Unit 36 貧窮的

StringNet語料庫出現次數

poor	impoverished	needy	destitute
15659	335	252	130

poor (adj.)

❖ 例句

In this country the gap between rich and **poor** is considerably wider than it was 20 years ago.

這國家的貧富差距比二十年前擴大許多。

❖ 常用搭配詞

poor + <u>n.</u>

country, people, man, area, region, state, neighborhood, child, farmer, peasant, harvest, class, economy, immigrant.

needy (adj.)

❖ 例句

The government provides free air transportation to **needy** medical patients.

這政府提供有需要的病人免費的空中交通。

❖ 常用搭配詞

needy + _n._

   family, people, year, child, folk, population, country, student, community, circumstance.

impoverished (adj.)

❖ 例句

He grew up with little formal education due to his **impoverished** childhood.
他由於童年窮苦，沒有受過很多正式教育。

❖ 常用搭配詞

impoverished + _n._

   family, area, people, child, country, community, neighborhood, region, life, condition, nation, farmer, state, peasant, immigrant, city, childhood, youth.

destitute (adj.)

❖ 例句

The church fed thousands of **destitute** people after the war.
戰後教會提供食物給數以千計飢餓的人群。

❖ 常用搭配詞

destitute + <u>n.</u>

child, people, life, worker, time, refugee, family, orphan.

綜合整理

poor	強調缺乏，可接與金錢或物資有關如economy或harvest的名詞。
needy	強調有需要，不見得都是物資缺乏，如needy patients，也可能是一段暫時的需要（如throughout the hungry and needy years）。
impoverished	後面可接childhood或youth表示一段貧窮的人生階段。
destitute	後面名詞多半是人物（如orphan, refugee），可指負面因素如戰爭等造成的貧窮。

poor, needy,和impoverished後面名詞可以是人物（如people, family）或地區（如country, community）。

Unit 37 品味、品嘗

StringNet語料庫出現次數

taste	relish
4088 (n.), 1417 (v.)	5410 (v.), 217 (n.)

taste (n.)

❖ 例句

He developed a **taste** for wine while staying with his grandfather.

他在和爺爺住的時候發展出對酒的興趣。

She has good **taste** in clothes.

她對服裝的品味很高。

❖ 常用搭配詞

develop/ acquire/ have a taste for + n.

history, study, bowling, sport, power, reading, wine, alcohol, performing in public, showbiz, language, reform, travel, poetry, card, figure, nut, adventure.

taste (vt.)

❖ 常用句型

> **S + taste + O**

❖ 例句

One year later she **tasted** her first success in a national piano competition.
一年之後她在一場全國鋼琴比賽中第一次嘗到成功的滋味。

❖ 常用搭配詞

taste + <u>n.</u>

　wine, blood, success, food, bitterness, death, fruit, defeat.

relish (n.)

❖ 例句

The hungry children ate the cake with great **relish**.
這些飢餓的孩子吃蛋糕吃得津津有味。

❖ 常用搭配詞

<u>v.</u> + with relish

　say, accept, eat, add, gossip.

relish (vt.)

❖ 常用句型

> **S + relish + O**

❖ 例句

Most people do not **relish** the idea of traveling alone.
大部分人不喜歡獨自旅行。

❖ 常用搭配詞

relish + (det.) _n._

  idea, story, challenge, thought, companionship, company, sound, prospect, role, look, thrill, decision, intervention.

綜合整理

taste	可當及物動詞或不及物動詞，在此只包含及物動詞，表示品嘗，後面名詞可接具體的食物或抽象的人生經驗（如success, defeat），當名詞時表示品味，也就是個人喜好或美學上的鑑賞力，與判斷力有關。
relish	當動詞時表示喜愛某件尚未或即將發生的事，常接否定表示不喜歡，當名詞也表示喜愛，和taste不同，與判斷力無關，受詞不能是人。with relish表示津津有味。

Unit 38 平等的、公平的

StringNet語料庫出現次數

fair	equal	egalitarian
8339	5951	259

fair (adj.)

❖ 例句

He deserved a **fair** trial even though he was a bandit.
縱然他是個惡棍，還是有權利接受公平的審判。

❖ 常用搭配詞

fair + n.

trading, share, amount, play, trial, price, deal, comment, chance, game, way, degree, competition, distribution, proportion, point, treatment, sex, market, society, exchange, voting, wage, test, comparison, opportunity, criticism, labelling, access, taxation, compensation, allocation, judgement.

equal (adj.)

❖ 例句

equal pay for equal work
同工同酬。

❖ 常用搭配詞

equal + n.

　opportunities, pay, terms, rights, treatment, access, status, footing, importance, basis, chance, distribution, share, right, proportion, representation, work, society, attention, protection, standing, conditions, citizenship, members, care, relationship, justice, respect, priority, points, sex, participation, exchange, voting, liberty, republics, competition, benefits, union, member, recognition, authority, responsibilities, nations.

egalitarian (adj.)

❖ 例句

Living in an **egalitarian** society, we enjoy equal opportunities of jobs and education.

我們住在平等的社會，享有公平的工作機會和教育機會。

❖ 常用搭配詞

egalitarian + n.

　society, feminists, feminism, approach, doctrine, distribution, vision, ideals, theory, notions, family, way, taxation, policies, education, ideas, principle.

綜合整理

fair	每個人受到相同待遇。
equal	人人享有平等的權利，機會、地位等。
egalitarian	平等主義的，人人生而平等，享有平等的權利。

Unit 39 平常的

StringNet語料庫出現次數

common	normal	usual	ordinary	typical
18890	12127	7305	6659	4757

common (adj.)

❖ 例句

Taxis are also a **common** form of transportation in the city.
計程車也是這個都市常見的交通工具。

❖ 常用搭配詞

common + <u>n.</u>

　　law, name, use, type, form, usage, cause, people, example, way, method, language, term, knowledge, school, reason, factor, sense, design, market, part, citizen, side-effect, person, people, position, life.

normal (adj.)

❖ 例句

The blind mother gave birth to a healthy, **normal** baby.
這位瞎眼的母親生下一個健康正常的嬰孩。

❖ 常用搭配詞

normal + n.

school, life, form, distribution, operation, human, condition, circumstance, level, mode, range, size, people, state, function, cell, time, use, practice, development, speed, part, level, user, functioning, route, procedure, behavior, day, blood, temperature, number, matter, relationship, environment.

usual (adj.)

❖ 例句

He went home earlier than **usual**.
他比平常早回家。
Meet me at the **usual** place after class.
下課後在老地方和我見面。

❖ 常用搭配詞

usual + n.

way, practice, sense, form, method, suspect, rule, style, term, definition, case, number, meaning, convention, name, order, procedure, type, role, course, format, time, range, target, response, reason, cause.

ordinary (adj.)

❖ 例句

Members of the royal family are not supposed to marry **ordinary** people.
皇室的成員被認為不應該和平民結婚。

❖ 常用搭配詞

ordinary + _n._

people, citizen, language, human, life, person, user, time, matter, course, soldier, sense, day, law, level, income, meaning, speech, moral, circumstance, world, computer, object, water, skill, school, household, worker, court, guy.

typical (adj.)

❖ 例句

The English teacher introduced **typical** foods for Thanksgiving.
這英文老師介紹典型的感恩節食物。

❖ 常用搭配詞

typical + _n._

example, performance, use, feature, application, day, form, case, service, design, style, year, size, home, pattern, family, method, adult, user, response, way, usage, food, show, member, computer, plot, speed, situation, problem, length, behavior, price, view, reaction, music, event, activity, definition, number, type.

綜合整理

common	表示常見的或經常發生的，相對於rare（罕見的）。
normal	表示正常的或符合預期的，相對於abnormal（反常的）。
usual	表示慣常的或在通常的時間或情況下發生的，如老地方（the usual place）和老時間（the usual time），相對於unusual（奇特的、稀有的）。
ordinary	表示普通的、不特別的，相對於extraordinary（超乎尋常的、非凡的）。
typical	表示典型的，一個族群中具有代表性的，相對於atypical（非典型的、反常的、不合規則的），untypical（非典型的），unique（獨特的），和unusual（奇特的、稀有的）。

基本上common和ordinary都強調和一般大眾一樣的、常見的，而typical、normal和usual則強調符合某種預期的典型或狀態，但是usual後面的名詞通常不是人，而typical和normal則可以接人。

Unit 40 平靜、冷靜

StringNet語料庫出現次數

peaceful	calm	tranquil	serene
1594	1277	299	210

peaceful (adj.)

❖ 例句

They cherish the **peaceful** life they have after all the trials and tribulations.
他們很珍惜這經過許多苦難之後才得到的平靜生活。

❖ 常用搭配詞

peaceful + n.

resolution, coexistence, life, mean, protest, solution, relation, settlement, demonstration, world, way, people, place, transition, revolution, method, existence, time, town, death, society, negotiation, planet, contact, area, community, environment, resistance, nature, election, manner, atmosphere, country, setting, retirement, year, land, condition, situation, moment.

calm (adj.)

❖ 例句

The captain told the passengers to stay calm and prepare before the emergency landing.
機長告訴乘客保持冷靜，準備迫降。

❖ 常用搭配詞

(det.) _n._ + be + calm

　　night, ocean, face, horizontal line, voice, soldier, community, station, love, mood, day, water, morning, greeting, tone, river, child.

calm + _n._

　　water, sea, weather, land, day, temperament, demeanor, condition, atmosphere, manner, mind, wind, disposition, night, time, nature, environment, air, period, discussion, moment, style, attitude, river, life, area, voice, city, mood, melody, tone, personality, heart, response, day, leader, member.

tranquil (adj.)

❖ 例句

They moved to a **tranquil** town after their retirement.
他們退休後搬到一個寧靜的小鎮。

❖ 常用搭配詞

tranquil + _n._

　　setting, place, life, period, environment, response, mind, atmosphere, response, spot, opening, garden, town, beauty, surrounding, scene, nature, galaxy, melody, water, behavior, lake, planet, haven, moment, position, demeanor, corner, picture, day, feeling, background, retirement.

serene (adj.)

❖ 例句

He was drawn to the priest's **serene** wisdom and decided to accept Christianity.

他被那位牧師沉靜的智慧所吸引，決定接受基督教。

❖ 常用搭配詞

serene + n.

girl, man, regard, letter, landscape, wisdom, face, progress, timelessness, lifestyle, island, delight, lake, rationality, calm, beauty, city, detachment, spirit, confidence, photograph, temperament, water, look, faith, acceptance, assurance, smile, optimism, welcome, commentary, scene.

綜合整理

peaceful	除了平靜還有則強調和平，沒有戰亂或憂慮的意思，後面接的名詞意義多樣化（例如peaceful coexistence和平共處）。
calm	這個字的意思強調在急難中仍保持冷靜，如stay後面可以接calm而不會接tranquil或serene。
tranquil	不但是平靜還有愉悅的含意，後面名詞很少是人。
serene	表示不受干擾。

calm, serene, 和tranquil意思相近，後面的名詞也很相似，可能是心情（例如feeling、mind）、地方（例如island、city）、時間（例如moment、life）、狀態（例如condition、retirement）或水面（例如river、lake）。

Unit 41 評估

StringNet語料庫出現次數

assess	estimate	evaluate	appraise
6347	5052	2422	259

assess (vt.)

❖ 常用句型

> S + assess + O
> S + be assessed as + N
> S + be assess at + N

❖ 例句

The hospital has various kinds of medical equipment to **assess** the health of new born babies.
這醫院有各種醫療設備來評估新生兒的健康。

Teachers can use a checklist to **assess** student success with a particular teaching material.
老師在使用新教材時可以用一種清單來評估學生的成功情形。

❖ 常用搭配詞

assess + (det.) <u>n.</u>

performance, impact, number, age, amount, significance, IQ, standard, ratio, status, force, nature, character, effect, incidence, response, quality, role, importance, size, article, situation, risk, level, need, health, progress, ability, condition, state, validity, feasibility, outcome, probability, result, skill, extent.

estimate (vt.)

❖ 常用句型

> **S + estimate + O**
> **S + estimate + that 子句**
> **S + be estimated + to Vroot**
> **S + be estimated at/ by + N**

❖ 常用句型

The population of this village **is estimated at** 2,000 people.
這村莊的人口估計約二千人。

Property damage caused by this typhoon was **estimated** around five hundred million dollars.
這次颱風造成的財物損失估計約有五億元。

❖ 常用搭配詞

(det.) _n._ +be estimated

population, damage, age, number, value, losses, equation, death toll, strength, traffic, total force, total viewership, repairs, input, debt, family assets, turnover, cost, damage.

evaluate (vt.)

❖ 常用句型

> **S + evaluate + O**

❖ 例句

After one year, the school **evaluated** the success of the new teaching method.
一年後這學校評估這種新教學方法的成效。

The way the school evaluates students for assigning rank is unfair.
這學校給學生排名次的評量方法不公平。

❖ 常用搭配詞

evaluate + (det.) _n._

information, impact, use, system, character, world, project, effectiveness, evidence, program, quality, development, success, contribution, learning, reliability, introduction, progress, expression, student, patient, risk, work, value, argument, model, situation, result, ability, claim, number, function, research, article, system, position.

appraise (vt.)

❖ 常用句型

> **S + appraise + O**

❖ 例句

The university introduces new measures to **appraise** the teachers'
performance.
這大學推出新的教師表現評鑑方法。

❖ 常用搭配詞

appraise + (det.) <u>n.</u>

performance, partnership, progress, teacher, figure, applicants, minister,
project, reply, motive, situation, achievement, plant, equipment, antique,
staff.

綜合整理

assess	表示計算價值、數量或重要性等，尤其是和課稅有關，也可以指經過深思熟慮後對一個人或一種情況做出判斷，和judge相等。
estimate	粗略估計價值、大小、或速度等，常用被動語態，後面可以接that子句用在發表意見。
evaluate	是判斷一件事物的成敗、用處、或優劣的程度，是經過仔細評量，和estimate粗略估計不同，受詞可以是人。
appraise	是正式用語，和evaluate意義相似。表示針對某事情的價值、成敗、及效果給予正式或官方的判斷，受詞可以是人，表示評斷其表現；也可以是物（例如古董或財物），表示估算其價值。在文學上也可以指審視的眼神。

Unit 42 評論

StringNet語料庫出現次數

comment	remark	commentary
7070	2977	943

comment (n.)

❖ 例句

His divorce received much negative **comment** in the public.

社會大眾對於他的離婚給予負面的批評。

❖ 常用搭配詞

 adj. + comment

further, subsequent, unsigned, public, negative, personal, previous, derogatory, many, racialist, critical, controversial, fair, sarcastic, positive, abusive, general, early, political, recent, rude, outside, anonymous, satirical, constructive, irrelevant, original, favorable, appropriate, offensive, editorial, inflammatory, official, humorous, insulting, social, uncivil, anti-Semitic, brief, insight, witty, adverse, nasty, derisive, ironic, harsh, hostile.

commentary (n.)

❖ 例句

They listened to the running **commentary** of the baseball game through the radio.

他們從收音機聽這場棒球比賽的實況報導。

❖ 常用搭配詞

adj. + commentary

social, audio, political, DVD, critical, extensive, biblical, many, detailed, daily, early, weekly, modern, humorous, brief, historical, regular, insightful, official, satirical, sarcastic, editorial, scholarly, ironic, personal, running.

remark (n.)

❖ 例句

His humorous **remarks** make him a popular lecturer.

他的風趣言論使他成為受歡迎的講師。

❖ 常用搭配詞

adj. + remark

respectful, rude, funny, silly, disparaging, idiotic, unflattering, critical, snide, vicious, juvenile, concerned, friendly, sardonic, obscene, racist, sexist, personal.

綜合整理

comment	指對某人的言語或行為發表的個人意見。
remark	指在正式演講所說的評論。
commentary	指書評，也就是解析或討論某一本書、某一首詩、或某一種思想的書籍或文章。另外也表示在收音機或電視等實況轉播時的播報評論。

commentary和**comment**可當可數或不可數名詞，**remark**則是可數名詞。

Unit 43 普遍的

StringNet語料庫出現次數

general	common	universal	prevalent
33626	18890	2531	521

general (adj.)

❖ 例句

There is a **general** lack of premarital education in our senior high schools.
我們的高中學校普遍缺乏婚前教育。

❖ 常用搭配詞

general + n.

election, library, hospital, staff, manager, secretary, rule, purpose, term, public, court, law, strike, counsel, office, government, convention, population, consensus, principle, sense, concept, knowledge, agreement, worker, theory, headquarter, idea, case, type, guideline, usage, interest, information, education, entertainment, solution, lack, trend, direction, policy, audience, view, classification.

common (adj.)

❖ 例句

This book provides solutions to **common** problems in communication.
這本書為常見的溝通問題提供解決方法。

❖ 常用搭配詞

common + _n._

problem, interest, misconception, belief, sense, knowledge, law, market, development, public, cold, routine, license, education.

universal (adj.)

❖ 例句

The topic of this novel has **universal** appeal.
這本書的主題符合大眾的喜好。

❖ 常用搭配詞

universal + _n._

suffrage, contempt, applause, derision, resentment, consternation, support, acceptance, assumption, resistance, feature, reaction, impression, factor, failure, experience, level, policy, source, practice, loss, ignorance, meaning, standard, tendency, delight, refusal, influence, cry, characteristics, use, law, condemnation, problem, disagreement, approval, belief.

prevalent (adj.)

❖ 例句

Currently English is the most **prevalent** language for communication on the Internet.
目前英文是網路上最普遍使用的語言。

❖ 常用搭配詞

prevalent + n.

form, view, theory, idea, use, language, practice, theme, opinion, ancestor, notion, disease, style, version, method, attitude, belief, system, species, feature, source, character, term, example, misconception, speculation, tendency.

綜合整理

general	(1)指牽涉某個情況、群體、或事物全面的，而非片面的（例如general health, general election）；(2)存在於或影響大多數人的（例如general interest）；(3)以及一般的，而非針對某種用途或活動等（例如general court)。
universal	有二個意義：一是與全世界或某群體中每一個個體有關的（universal interest），和general相似；二是放諸四海皆準的（universal truth）。
common	指普通的或普遍存在的（例如common knowledge）。
prevalent	指廣泛地發生、存在、接受、或流行的。

Unit 44 模式

StringNet語料庫出現次數

pattern	mode
14622	3918

pattern (n.)

❖ 例句

He tried to detect the **pattern** of the sound change in the unknown language.
他試著找出這未知語言聲音改變的模式。

❖ 常用搭配詞

pattern of + (det.) <u>n.</u>

trade, sound change, terrorist activity, gene, expression, energy deposition, trading-off, rural decline, sound, gesture, alternation, dates, thought, feeling, behavior, inheritance, use and abandonment, series, harassment, village life, misjudgment, growth, movement, production, argument, global warming, fashion, activity, system, conduct, language, genetic control, migration, relationship, progress, regress.

mode (n.)

❖ 例句

He is profoundly influenced by Western **modes of** thought.
他深受西方思想模式的影響。
In the city buses are the most efficient **mode of** transport.
這個城市裡公車是效率最高的交通工具。

❖ 常用搭配詞

mode of + (det.) _n._

communication, transport, operation, treatment, transmission, production, speech, computer hardware and software, travel, failure, design, design-method, inquiry, road transport, transportation, oscillation, lower frequency, measured system, measuring apparatus, atom, Window 95, dress, possible change, reasoning, moviemaking, occurrence, thought, political direction, religion, play, life, game, advertising, attention, action, statement, response, corruption, appointing, death, music, disposal, election, growth, interaction.

綜合整理

pattern	一件事情固定的，規律發生的（regular）模式，例如在一些不規則的事物中找出其中的規律性，或重複的圖案。
mode	指的是某一特殊的、特定的行動或行為模式，通常是指許多同類中的其中一種，例如modes of transport是指各種交通方式。

Unit 45 摩擦

StringNet語料庫出現次數

rub	friction
2113	504

rub (vi. / vt.)

❖ 常用句型

> **S + rub + O**
> **S + rub + O + with/ against/ on + N**
> **S + rub + prep. + O**

❖ 例句

My cat purred and **rubbed** her head against my legs when I came home.
當我回家時我的貓一邊呼嚕叫一邊用她的頭摩蹭我的腿。

❖ 常用搭配詞

rub + (det.) _n._

eyes, face, nose, hands, surface, wings, ashes, oil, back, lamp, stomach, belly, skin.

friction (n.)

❖ 例句

His dominant attitude is often the cause of **friction** between him and his co-workers.

他的強勢態度時常造成他和同事之間的摩擦。

The shoes are designed for high **friction** with the pedals of the pipe organ.

這鞋子是為了和管風琴踏板經常摩擦而設計的。

❖ 常用搭配詞

<u>adj.</u> + friction

internal, static, much, considerable, political, high, kinetic, atmospheric, constant, dynamic, economic, minimal, cultural, reduced, unnecessary, small, little.

<u>v.</u> + friction

cause, reduce, increase, minimize, provide, generate, result in, delete, produce, avoid, prevent.

綜合整理

rub	可當作動詞和名詞，指的是物體之間的摩擦，表示擦式、摩擦、按摩、磨損、或擦傷。rub較常當作動詞，可加上名詞形成成語如rub shoulders with（與……有來往）、rub salt in/ into one's wound(s)（在傷口上灑鹽巴）、rub someone the wrong way（激怒，惹怒）；rub當名詞時雖也可指人際關係的摩擦，但不常用。
friction	只當名詞用，可以指人與人之間關係上的摩擦和物體之間的摩擦，但前者較常用，表示衝突。

Unit 46 買

StringNet語料庫出現次數

buy	purchase
25567 (v.), 257 (n.)	3833 (v.), 3833 (n.)

buy (vi. / vt.)

❖ 常用句型

> **S + buy somebody something**
> **S + buy something for somebody**
> **S + buy something for 價錢**
> **S + buy (+ O) + prep. + N**

❖ 例句

He **bought** his wife a castle in the country.

他在鄉下為他妻子買了一棟城堡。

They seldom **buy** with credit cards.

他們很少用信用卡購物。

❖ 常用搭配詞

buy + (det.) _n._

land, right, house, share, company, time, ticket, property, stock, car, station, product, home, goods, book, team, equipment, weapon, building, asset, island, newspaper, service, license, insurance.

buy (n.)

❖ 例句

Smart phones continued to be a popular **buy**.
智慧型手機的銷路依然熱絡。
The second-hand Mercedez looks like a good **buy**.
這輛二手賓士車看起來很划算。

❖ 常用搭配詞

adj. + buy

good, best, better, popular, recommended, second-hand, excellent, shrewd, expensive, attractive, possible, strong, bad, latest.

purchase (vt.)

❖ 常用句型

S + purchase + O (+ prep. + N)

❖ 例句

There is a trend among the celebrity to **purchase** coastal properties as a secondary homes.
名人很流行買海邊別墅。

❖ 常用搭配詞

purchase + (det.) n.

property, right, company, house, share, station, land, ticket, goods, equipment, building, estate, home, product, service, team, asset, island, farm, stock, license, food, weapon, insurance, slave.

purchase (n.)

❖ 例句

House **purchase** seems impossible for young couples due to the skyrocketing house prices.
由於房價太高，年輕夫婦不可能買得起房子。

❖ 常用搭配詞

adj. + purchase

compulsory, outright, original, proposed, initial, recent, joint, major, possible, each, new, direct, full, individual, private, expensive, off-market, minimum, intended, future, particular, essential, special, subsequent, planned, final, industria, potential, total, actual, prospective, simple, exclusive, worthwhile, agreed, attractive, good, big, early, continued, specific, small, various, commercial, annual, low, forward, extravagant, firm, excellent, deferred, single, paid.

綜合整理

buy	可當及物或不及物動詞，也可當授與動詞後面接直接受詞和間接受詞（例如She bought her son a motorcycle./ She bought a motorcycle for her son.），buy也有其他意思如相信（例如buy the story）和爭取緩衝時間（例如He tried to buy himself more time by telling a white lie.）。當名詞表示價廉物美、值得購買的商品。
purchase	是正式用字，只能當及物動詞。當名詞時表示購買行為或購買的商品。

Unit 47 媒體

StringNet語料庫出現次數

press	media
10105	7837

press (n.)

❖ 例句

The tabloid **press** was once called "yellow journalism."

八卦小報曾經被稱為「黃色新聞業」。

❖ 常用搭配詞

press + n.

conference, release, officer, coverage, reports, office, association, freedom, attention, article, statement, interview, photographer, briefing, agency, award, newspaper, time, gallery, page, photograph, agent, comic, group, publisher, baron, reporter, interest, censorship, magazine, law, campaign, announcement, information, source, event, image, show.

adj. + press

small, British, local, national, popular, tabloid, international, free, bad, mainstream, negative, official, various, underground, foreign, amateur, scholastic, daily, original, positive, western, academic, public, online, contemporary.

media (n.)

❖ 例句

The murder crime has become a **media** event.
這樁謀殺犯罪被媒體大肆報導。

❖ 常用搭配詞

media + n.

attention, coverage, spotlight, interest, relation, circus, hype, study, campaign, report, people, education, product, device, omnipotence, list, people, planner, item, unit, type, baron, proprietor, mogul.

adj. + media

online, transcontinental, Canadian, instructional.

綜合整理

press	有印刷的意思，因此較偏重平面媒體（如報紙和雜誌）及平面媒體的內容，由於早期的新聞以平面媒體為主，因此press常出現在與新聞業相關的專門用語，例如新聞自由（**press freedom**）和新聞審查（**press censorship**）等。
media	意義比較廣，代表所有媒體，所以有**press and other media**的用法，過去使用的**press baron**也逐漸被**media baron**所取代，指藉著擁有媒體而加以壟斷操控的人，類似的新專門用語有**media mogul**、或**media proprietor**。另外**media**也常用來表示新聞從業人員的活動，如**media circus**是嘲諷媒體人員一窩蜂報導某件事情，而這種過度報導的現象被稱為**media hype**。

Unit 48 魅力

StringNet語料庫出現次數

appeal	charm	charisma	allure
10378	1451	224	64

appeal (n.)

❖ 例句

Jeremy Lin's story has received international **appeal**.
林書豪的故事風靡各國。

❖ 常用搭配詞

<u>adj.</u> + appeal

commercial, popular, aesthetic, wide, public, personal, visual, emotional, international, broad, great, mass, universal, widespread, mainstream, sexual, enduring, charismatic, artistic.

charm (n.)

❖ 例句

she visited that town every year for its rural **charm**.
她因為喜歡那個小鎮的鄉間風味每年都去造訪。

❖ 常用搭配詞

adj. + charm

personal, fatal, great, rural, boyish, unique, natural, special, magical, rustic, small-town, original, picturesque, Victorian, historical, traditional.

charisma (n.)

❖ 例句

His personal **charisma** made him the most popular basketball player on the school team.

他的個人魅力使他成為學校籃球校隊最受歡迎的球員。

❖ 常用搭配詞

adj. + charisma

personal, natural, special, great, unique, strong, individual, sexual, royal.

allure (n.)

❖ 例句

He had been drawn by the **allure** of rock-climbing and eventually died when he was climbing the Great Canyon.

他對攀岩深深著迷,最後在攀登大峽谷時死亡。

❖ 常用搭配詞

adj. + allure

sexual, breathtaking.

綜合整理

appeal	使人喜歡上的特質，可以形容人或非人。因為當名詞時還有其他意義，因此在語料庫出現次數較多。
charm	使人喜歡上或被影響的特質，可以形容人或非人。
charisma	指天生、自然而成的魅力，只用來形容人。
allure	所指的魅力帶有神祕、刺激的含意，可以形容人或非人。

Unit 49 冒犯

StringNet語料庫出現次數

offend	insult	affront
931	438	72

offend (vt.)

❖ 常用句型

> **S + offend + O**
> **S + be offend at/by something**

❖ 例句

The guest was **offended by** the host's negligence.
這位客人對主人的忽視感到生氣。

❖ 常用搭配詞

be offended by + (det.) _n._

attitude, sight, refusal, brutality, suggestion, work, channel, breach, criticism, material, comparison, interest, charm, language, defiance, obsession, negligence, bluntness, fascination, attack, people, sex scene, low rank.

insult (vt.)

❖ 常用句型

> **S + insult + O**
> **S + insult somebody by doing something**

❖ 例句

His remarks have **insulted** the integrity of the Ministry of the Justice.
他的言論侮辱了司法部的廉明。

❖ 常用搭配詞

be insulted by + (det.) <u>n.</u>

expert, fashion arbiter, anything one might say, decay, offer, smell, Spanish, weakness.

insult + (det.) <u>n.</u>

intelligence, queen, English, guy, media, God, memory, lot, woman, man, kid, contestant, donation, cook, integrity, weather, head, honor, state flag, leader, passer-by.

affront (vt. / n.)

❖ 例句

He felt **affronted** by her refusal to his proposal.

他對她拒絕他的求婚感到被侮辱。

It is an intolerable affront to her pride.

這是對她的自尊不可忍受的侮辱。

❖ 常用搭配詞

be affronted by + (det.) _n._

　pretension, failure, frankness, impact, familiarity, lack of respect, extremity, question, publication.

綜合整理

offend	因粗魯、不友善的言語或行為有意或無意使人生氣、反感、不悅、或受傷，主動和被動的用法都常見，受詞通常是人。
insult	較常用主動語態，表示藉由傲慢、漠視、或輕視等無禮的行為而蓄意造成的冒犯，主動和被動的用法都常見，受詞可以是人或非人。
affront	表示公開、蓄意的冒犯侮辱，常當作名詞或動詞被動語態。

Unit 50 模糊的、不清楚的

StringNet語料庫出現次數

faint	vague	dim	hazy	fuzzy	blurred	indistinct
1758	1442	670	234	187	135	103

faint (adj.)

❖ 例句

He saw a **faint** light in the darkness.
他看到黑暗中有微弱的光線。

❖ 常用搭配詞

faint + n.

light, noise, idea, hope, smile, possibility, chance, sound, trace, track, path, humming, scent, illusion, glimmer, smell, memory, mark.

vague (adj.)

❖ 例句

Most people have a **vague** understanding of the new policy.
大多數人對這個新政策瞭解不清。

❖ 常用搭配詞

vague + <u>n.</u>

way, recollection, idea, connection, sense, thought, notion, promise, fancy, understanding, question, impression, noise, aspiration, anxiety, memory, pledge, hint, brief, discussion, remark, feeling, consensus, description, comment.

dim (adj.)

❖ 例句

He couldn't see clearly in the **dim** light.
在黯淡的光中他看不清楚。

❖ 常用搭配詞

dim + <u>n.</u>

glow, light, shape, outline, room, bathroom, interior, candle light, distance, view, grasp, recollection, awareness, memory.

hazy (adj.)

❖ 例句

He had only a **hazy** recollection of his mother.
他對他的母親只有模糊的回憶。

hazy + n.

  sunshine, mirage, area, idea, image, sun, day, understanding, notion, morning, memory, dream, recollection, halo, curtain.

fuzzy (adj.)

❖ 例句

There is a **fuzzy** line between madness and genius.
瘋狂與天才之間的界線模糊。

❖ 常用搭配詞

fuzzy + n.

  line, image, voice, system, rule, logic, photograph, edge, mind, eye, indistinctness, focus, account, background, patch, vision, blankness, figure, information, definition, data.

blurred (adj.)

❖ 例句

He was looking at the **blurred** photos of his parents' wedding.
他看著那些模糊不清的他父母的結婚照。

❖ 常用搭配詞

blurred + n.

  photo, memory, outline, inscription, landscape, thumbprint, shape, form, view, impression, voice, mist, glimpse, flurry.

indistinct (adj.)

❖ 例句

An **indistinct** figure walked out from the fog.
一個模糊的身影從霧中走出來。

❖ 常用搭配詞

indistinct + n.

figure, voice, background, analysis, path, gunfire, action, image, line, mutter, contrast, signal, sound, scale, object, shape, murmur.

綜合整理

faint	表示難以用感官視聽聞到，微弱的，絲毫的（如faint hope/chance）。
vague	指的是形狀不清楚（=indistinct）或細節不清楚。
dim	指因光線太暗模糊（如a dim glow）也可形容記憶或想法（如dim recollection / awareness）。
hazy	表示因灰塵、煙霧等造成的模糊（如hazy sunshine），或不清楚或不確定的記憶或想法。
fuzzy	等於blurred，表示不清楚、界限不明（二者易混淆）。
blurred	等於fuzzy，表示不清楚、界限不明（二者易混淆）。
indistinct	表示模糊、難以辨識的，如聲音、影像、或記憶。

Unit 51 蹣跚、搖搖欲墜

StringNet語料庫出現次數

falter	wobble	totter	waddle	toddle	dodder
403	220	154	96	45	29

falter (vi.)

❖ 例句

The old man **faltered** at the sight of his long-lost son.
那位老先生看到失散多年的兒子時幾乎站立不住。

❖ 常用搭配詞

(det.) n. + falter

voice, smile, step, man, growth, stride, tone, campaign, confidence, explanation, heart, economy, footstep, reform, authority, empire.

wobble (vi.)

❖ 例句

to **wobble** around on one's bike/ high heels
騎在腳踏車上（穿著高跟鞋）搖搖晃晃
wobble like a jelly
像果凍般搖搖晃晃

❖ 常用搭配詞

(det.) _n._ + wobble

  leg, ball, glass, body, car, mass, stool, plane, vessel, knee, head, chin.

totter (vi.)

❖ 例句

to **totter** precariously/unsteadily
搖搖欲墜
to **totter** down the road
蹣跚而行

❖ 常用搭配詞

(det.) _n._ + totter

men, people, England, mummy, veteran, leg, child, country, reputation.

waddle (vi.)

❖ 例句

to **waddle** out of the room
搖搖擺擺地走出房間
to **waddle** down the passage
搖搖擺擺地沿著通道走

❖ 常用搭配詞

(det.) _n._ + waddle

  geese, duck, outgoer, man.

toddle (vi.)

❖ 例句

to **toddle** off like a drunk

像醉漢一般東倒西歪地走開

to **toddle** back to the office

東倒西歪地走回辦公室

❖ 常用搭配詞

(det.) _n._ + toddle

  baby, he, I.

dodder (vi.)

❖ 例句

a **doddering** old woman

步履艱難的老太太

綜合整理

falter	因為突然感到虛弱或害怕而停下腳步或步伐不穩。另外也可以指人說話吞吞吐吐不確定、信念動搖、或某制度或組織式微沒落。
wobble	因為不平衡而左右搖晃，可以指人的身體部位或堆高物品。
totter	左右搖晃劇烈，幾乎要倒下，例如酒醉後走路。
waddle	步伐小，身體左右搖晃，尤其是人或鳥禽類身體肥胖而腿短的走路模樣。
toddle	指小孩學走路時步伐小而不穩定，在英式英文中也指很悠哉地散步。
dodder	輕微搖晃，但步履艱難，如老人走路。在StringNet語料庫中沒有收錄句子。

Unit 52 滿足

StringNet語料庫出現次數

satisfy	content	gratify
2833	1498	138

satisfy (vt.)

❖ 常用句型

> **S + satisfy + O**

❖ 例句

Don't **satisfy** your curiosity at the expense of the privacy of other people.

不要為了滿足自己的好奇心而犧牲別人的隱私。

❖ 常用搭配詞

satisfy + (det.) _n._

　　requirement, demands, curiosity, condition, need, criteria, wife, prisoner, appetite, court, standard, principle.

content (adj.)

❖ 常用句型

> **S + be content with + N/ Ving**
> **S + be content + to Vroot**

❖ 例句

She seems **content** to be a housewife.

她似乎滿足於當一個家庭主婦。

Without more fund, the researcher had to **be content with** the old computer equipment.

由於沒有更多經費，這研究人員只好將就著使用舊電腦設備。

❖ 常用搭配詞

be content with + (det./ adj.) n.

one child（數量+名詞）, lot, a substitute's role, style, possibility, view, mode, prize, minimum, place, honor, wife, life, ruling, film, thing, relationship, game, existence, movement, lot, publicity, phone call, status, rent, result, vice-presidency, advantage.

gratify (vt.)

❖ 常用句型

> S + gratify + O
> S + be gratified + to Vroot

❖ 例句

He **was gratified to** see his autobiography published.

他對於自傳的出版感到高興。

They **are gratified** by their children's devotion to the church.

他們對孩子們熱心貢獻教會感到欣慰。

❖ 常用搭配詞

be gratified by + (det./ adj.) <u>n.</u>

　　performance, rare sight, devotion, closeness, change, recognition, response, anger, question, anger, resistance, pledge, attempt, goodwill, friendship.

gratify + (det.) <u>n.</u>

　　curiosity, constituents, vanity, men, town, voter, wish.

綜合整理

satisfy	指(1)行為符合某人的期望而使之感到滿足，後面受詞是人或非人（例如to satisfy one's father, to satisfy one's curiosity）；(2)提供某種需要的事物，滿足某種要求（例如to satisfy the standard），此種用法類似meet和fulfill（如meet/ fulfill a requirement）。被動語態常用be satisfied with句型。
content	表示滿足於或安於某種作法或情況，不做更多努力。也常和have to一起用（have to be content with + Ving/n.），表示不得不將就某種作法或情況。
gratify	是正式用字，意思和satisfy (1)相近，但強調滿足的感受，也有欣慰的含意，常用被動be gratified by或be gratified to + v.句型。

Unit 53 謎

StringNet語料庫出現次數

mystery	puzzle	riddle	enigma
2681	686	189	245

mystery (n.)

❖ 例句

The cause of his death remains a **mystery**.
他的死因仍舊是個謎。

❖ 常用搭配詞

adj. + mystery

total, religious, complete, great, certain, peculiar, rigorous, magical, inexplicable, racing, enormous, big, contemporary, great, minor, considerable, real, atmospheric, major, fascinating.

puzzle (n.)

❖ 例句

The pieces of the jigsaw **puzzle** were jumbled together.
這拼圖的小片都混在一起。

❖ 常用搭配詞

adj. + puzzle

real, Chinese, botanical, theoretical, confound, baffling, scientific, intricate, complicated, great, famous, psychological, intriguing, considerable, typographical, small, biochemical, tough, mental, good, enormous, intellectual, giant, perfect, wooden, embarrassing.

riddle (n.)

❖ 例句

No one could solve the **riddle**.
沒有人能解開這個謎題。
Stop talking in **riddles**!
說話別打啞謎。

❖ 常用搭配詞

adj. + riddle

unsolved, hard, basic, ancient, simple, agonizing, this, famous, mysterious, little, whole, particular, fascinating, great.

enigma (n.)

❖ 例句

He is an **enigma** in the eyes of his classmates.
他在同學眼中是個謎樣的人物。

❖ 常用搭配詞

adj. + enigma

persistent, total, eternal, paleontological, veritable, present, this, important, fascinating, gorgeous, taxonomic, evolutionary, great, unsolvable, constant, extraordinary, total, sheer, accessible, famous.

綜合整理

mystery	和enigma相同，但比較常用，有奇怪、神秘的意思，可指人。
puzzle	常用在益智遊戲（crossword puzzles填字遊戲，tavern puzzle益智套環，Sudoku puzzles數獨）。
riddle	常指謎語，尤其是有機智或幽默的謎語。
enigma	和mystery相同，有奇怪、神秘的意思，可指人。

這四個字都指難以了解或解釋的事物，enigma和mystery指的多半是不可理解的，所以有remain a mystery/ remain an enigma的用法，而riddle和puzzle則指有解答的，所以常有solve the riddle/ puzzle的用法。

Unit 54 勉強的

StringNet語料庫出現次數

reluctant	unwilling
1946	964

reluctant (adj.)

❖ 例句

She gave him a **reluctant** smile.
她勉強地對他微笑。

❖ 常用搭配詞

reluctant + n.
   smile, acceptance, agreement.

unwilling (adj.)

❖ 例句

Most old people are **unwilling** to accept change.
大部分人都不願意接受改變。

❖ 常用搭配詞

unwilling + <u>n.</u>

farewell, player, bride, female, customer, victim, donor, party, patient, witness, majority, husband, host, dependence, hero.

綜合整理

reluctant	勉強的、拖拖拉拉的。常在後面加上不定詞片語（to-Vroot），有時候也會接名詞，但通常後面的名詞不能是人。
unwilling	勉強的、不甘情願的。常在後面加上不定詞片語（to-Vroot），有時候也會接名詞，而且後面的名詞通常是人。

Unit 55 面臨、面對

StringNet語料庫出現次數

face	confront
15861	2348

face (vt.)

❖ 常用句型

> S + face + O
> S + be faced with something

❖ 例句

They **have been faced with** various difficulties in the past few years.
在過去幾年中他們面對了各種困難。

One of the problems **facing** the new government is the racial conflict.
這新政府要面對的其中一個問題是種族衝突。

❖ 常用搭配詞

face up to + (det.) + <u>n.</u>
　　fact, reality, threat, question, boss, need, bureaucracy, confusion, way.

face (be faced with) + (det.) + <u>adj. + n.</u>
　　tiresome child, real world, superior horsepower, strong weight,
　　considerable barrage, unwanted takeover bid, blatant fact, passive

opposition, negative answer, hostile situation, difficult question, financial crisis, persistent problem.

face + _n._

charges, trial, south, problems, death, closure, prosecution, difficulties, facts, extinction, eviction, redundancy, life, starvation, opposition, competition, reality, fines, criticism, bankruptcy, women, ruin, England, defeat, demands, famine, questions, danger, people, pressure, deportation, action, challenges, hostility, losses, persecution, jail, front, chaos, teacher, re-election, rape, extradition, society, George, uncertainty, demolition, accusations, police, God, dismissal, unemployment, liquidation, battle, expulsion, changes, retirement.

(det.) + _n._ facing somebody

problems, dilemma, task, challenge, difficulties, dangers, recession.

confront (vt.)

❖ 常用句型

> **S + confront + O**
> **S + be confronted with something**

❖ 例句

Cats tend to be curious when **confronted with** moving objects.
貓看到移動的物體容易產生好奇心。

❖ 常用搭配詞

be confronted with + (det.) + <u>n.</u>

failure, situation, mystery, loss, deputation, decision, tourist, poverty, liqueur, argument, face, need, case, owner, problem, war, evidence, paradox, question, dilemma, aftermath, conflict.

綜合整理

face	表示面臨必須處理的困難，主動和被動的意義一樣（如He faced a dilemma. = He is faced with a dilemma.）。face也指面對、承認不想接受的現實（face up to），後面的受詞多半有負面的意義（如difficulty, challenge等）。
confront	表示面臨必須處理的困難，也有對抗、勇敢面對的意思。在語料庫中後面的受詞不一定有負面的意義。

Unit 56 名稱

StringNet語料庫出現次數

name	title	designation	denomination
31257	9841	418	377

name (n.)

❖ 例句

I can't remember the **name** of the company he is working at.
我想不起來他工作的公司的名字。

❖ 常用搭配詞

the name of + (det.) + n.

acid, work, company, newspaper, publication, species, individual, ship, abbey, sponsor, ancestor, Deity, soldier, jungle, crow, headquarter, position, a people, organization, clan, command, victim, taskforce, government, movement, flower, concentration camp, village, product, town, airport, character, team, font, ministry, subsidiary, act, recording, station, group, vessel, Internet, proposal, method, play, medication.

title (n.)

❖ 例句

She has watched so many films that she can't remember all of their **titles**.
她看過太多電影，以至於無法記得它們全部的名字。

❖ 常用搭配詞

the title of + (det.) + n.

film, edition, song, laureate, firm, album, article, show, work, novel, compilation, page, section, section, paper, rank, book, program, adventure, CD, state, source document, tribal official, piece, movie, job, position, image.

designation (n.)

❖ 例句

What is your official **designation** in the company?
你在這公司的正式職稱是甚麼？

❖ 常用搭配詞

n. + designation

highway, model, route, US, aircraft, number, type, letter, interstate, star, class, road, service, vehicle, unit, army, numeral, wilderness, area, official.

adj. + designation

official, provisional, military, new, numerical, temporary, original, territorial, geographical, racial, regimental, ethnic.

designation of + n.

areas, sites, assets.

denomination (n.)

❖ 例句

Christian of all **denominations** attended the conference.
各個教派的基督徒都來參加這個會議。

❖ 常用搭配詞

adj. + denomination

Christian, Protestant, religious, large, Jewish, various, small, Pentecostal, Presbyterian, Baptist, mainline, Evangelical, conservative, Mormon, reformed, official.

綜合整理

name	最常用，泛指一般人、動植物、公司、機構、船隻、地方等的名字。
title	通常是指書籍、戲劇、畫作、歌曲、文章等創作成品的名稱，以及階級、職位的名稱。
designation	指為區分眾多同類物件而編排的名稱，如公路、高速公路、軍事單位、飛機、星球、地理區域等，這些名稱有時會包含文字與數字，也可以指人的種族、職位的名稱。
denomination	大多用在宗教教派的名稱。

Unit 57 名聲、名譽

StringNet語料庫出現次數

reputation	fame
3847	1181

reputation (n.)

❖ 常用句型

> **S + has a reputation for something**
> **S + earn/gain/establish a reputation as something**

❖ 例句

He **has a reputation for** being bad-tempered.
他以壞脾氣著稱。

His achievements over the past years has earned him a **reputation as** a leading world authority on genetic engineering.
他在過去幾年的成就贏得了在遺傳工程上全球權威的名聲。

❖ 常用搭配詞

have a reputation for being + _adj._

　　tough, inclusive, helpful, elusive, reclusive, tender, difficult, devious, raucous, worthwhile, independent, bad-tempered.

adj. + reputation

international, good, bad, high, great, strong, excellent, poor, national, considerable, academic, solid, literary, fearsome, negative, notorious, worldwide, formidable, professional, well-deserved, undeserved, unsavory, outstanding, popular, public, infamous, artistic, global.

v. + one's reputation

make, establish, stake, enhance, build, do, restore, use, earn, save, increase, know, seal, damage, tarnish, confirm.

v. + a reputation

have, gain, acquire, establish, earn, build, develop, get, achieve, acquire, make, enjoy, garner.

fame (n.)

❖ 常用句型

> **S + rise/shoot to fame**

❖ 例句

He hasn't gotten used to the sudden **fame**.
他還沒習慣突然成名。
Eddie Redmayne **shot to fame** in 2015 when he won the Academy Award for Best Actor.
Eddie Redmayne贏得2015年奧斯卡最佳男演員後一炮而紅。

❖ 常用搭配詞

<u>adj.</u> + fame

international, great, national, worldwide, widespread, lasting, local, considerable, literary, instant, sudden, early, newfound, public, current, unexpected, immediate, eternal, musical, military, scientific, legendary, small.

<u>v.</u> + to fame

shoot, rise, come.

<u>v.</u> + fame

achieve, find, gain, win, seek, chase, bring.

綜合整理

repuation	因為過去發生某事而造成大眾對某人或某事的看法或意見，可能是好或壞的名聲，前面接的形容詞可能有正面或負面的意義（如negative reputation）或某個領域（如academic reputation等）的名聲。常用來表示長時間累積的行為或成就所帶來的名聲，前面可接動詞develop，這種名聲須要努力維持（如main/ protect one's reputation），不然會被破壞（如ruin/ tarnish one's reputation）。
fame	因某人的成就而得的名聲，前面接的形容詞大多有正面意義或某個領域（如scientific fame, literary fame等）的名聲。也常指突然來的名聲（如sudden/ immediate/ unexpected fame），時間上不見得持久，前面可用動詞rise或shoot表示一炮而紅（rise/shoot to fame）。

Unit 58 明白、瞭解

StringNet語料庫出現次數

understand	see	realize
226600	183800	5488

understand (vt.)

❖ 常用句型

> S + understand + O
> S + understand + that 子句
> S + understand + how/ why/ where etc. + 子句

❖ 例句

Many parents don't **understand** their children.

許多家長不了解他們的孩子。

I don't **understand why** he resigned from his position.

我不了解他為何辭去職位。

❖ 常用搭配詞

understand + (det.) <u>n.</u>

language, concept, term, nature, meaning, process, difference, word, people, importance, need, world, behavior, problem, God, way, reason, relationship, culture, principle, mindset, issue, situation, man, human, significance, text, change, value, effect, article, science, message, idea, mechanism, philosophy, literature, frustration, implication, law, anyone, logic, answer, joke.

see (vt.)

❖ 常用句型

> **S + see why/ how/ what etc. + 子句**

❖ 例句

I don't **see why** it doesn't work.
我不明白為何這樣做沒用。

❖ 常用搭配詞

not see any + _n._
　　reason, point, problem, sign, need, difference, police, prospect.

realize (vt.)

❖ 常用句型

> **S + realize + O**
> **S + realize who/ what/ how etc. +子句**
> **S + realize + that 子句**

❖ 例句

He suddenly **realized** the danger around him.
他突然察覺到周圍的危險。

We didn't **realize that** we were being followed.
我們沒有察覺自己被跟蹤了。

❖ 常用搭配詞

realize + (det.) n.

importance, truth, need, error, danger, value, extent, futility, situation, power, profit, plan, love, problem, necessity, benefit, threat, strength, advantage, feeling, opportunity, identity.

綜合整理

understand	表示明白別人說話的意義，明白某個事實、情況、或過程的基本運作，具有同理心而能瞭解某人的感受或行為。
see	指明白某事的進展、改變、或存在，或察覺某個事實。
realize	指明白某個情況或局勢的存在或嚴重性，以及意識或明白自己的處境，強調從不瞭解變為瞭解，有時候指突然間明白。

總而言之，understand範圍較廣，包含理智與情感上的瞭解，後面的受詞可以是人；realize和see比較偏向心智上的察覺，後面的受詞時常是抽象的名詞或子句解釋某個情況。

Unit 59 明亮的

StringNet語料庫出現次數

light	bright	brilliant	shining
22544	5270	3411	1150

light (adj.)

❖ 例句

We must do the work while it is still **light**.
我們要趁還有光線時趕快工作。

❖ 常用搭配詞

(det.) + _n._ + be light

　　room, saloon, furniture, garden, place, bedroom, evening, church, station, sky, background.

bright (adj.)

❖ 例句

Try to look at the **bright** side and be optimistic.
試著往好處想，樂觀一點。

❖ 常用搭配詞

bright + n.

　　light, color, future, star, eyes, spot, smile, side, sunlight.

bright + color + (n.)

　　red lipstick, yellow, yellow flowers.

(det.) + n. be bright (with + N.)

　　eyes, room, bedroom, color, sound, field, garden, road, turf, entrance, lobby, curtain, room, finger, place, day, weather, air, visage, appearance, Sunday, sun, plastic, house, voice, canvas.

brilliant (adj.)

❖ 例句

You look younger in **brilliant** color.
你穿亮色的衣服看起來比較年輕。

❖ 常用搭配詞

brilliant + n.

　　color, sunshine, star, smile, light, dawn, sun, spark, blue, white.

(det.) + n. + be brilliant

　　morning, sky.

shining (adj.)

❖ 例句

He was woken up by the **shining** morning sun.

他被早晨耀眼的陽光吵醒。

His eyes **shone** with excitement.

他的雙眼閃爍著興奮的光芒。

❖ 常用搭配詞

shining + n.

sun, moon, lamp, eyes, torch, beam.

n. + shine

sun, moon, light, star, eyes, laser, pool, stove, color, torch, lamp, window, river, landscape, sea, flood.

綜合整理

light	指白天的日光，室內（房間）光線充足，尤其是因日光照進來。
bright	指明亮或強烈刺眼的光，也可指出太陽時的強烈陽光。
brilliant	表示明亮的光或顏色，後面只接有關光線或顏色的名詞。另外有其他意義如優秀、有才華的、輝煌的。
shine	指物體本身所發出的亮光，是不及物動詞，最常見的主詞是自然光體（sun, moon, star）和eyes等。

Unit 60 命運、運氣

StringNet語料庫出現次數

fortune	luck	fate	destiny	predestination
2988	2907	2232	795	52

fortune (n.)

❖ 例句

I have the good **fortune** to live next to George William.
我有幸住在George William的隔壁。

❖ 常用搭配詞

<u>v.</u> + (det.) fortune

  seek, follow, change, revive, reverse, tell, improve,

luck (n.)

❖ 例句

Peter tried his **luck** in the big city.
Peter到大城市試運氣。

❖ 常用搭配詞

<u>v.</u> + (det.) fate

  try, curse, chance, push, believe, ride, share.

fate (n.)

❖ 片語

to leave one's fate to something or somebody
讓某人或某事決定某人的命運
to leave sb to his/ her fate
讓某人聽天由命

❖ 常用搭配詞

<u>v.</u> + (det.) fate

suffer, meet, seal, share, have, determine, escape, accept, avoid, learn, face, concern, discover, change, reveal, follow, find, control, regard, make, await, deserve, lament, describe, fear.

destiny (n.)

❖ 例句

It is your **destiny** to be a pianist.
你命中注定成為一位鋼琴家。

❖ 常用搭配詞

<u>v.</u> + (det.) destiny

fulfill, control, accept, shape, find, see, change, meet, determine, believe, create, seek.

綜合整理

fortune	可以指好或不好的命運，意義較中性，所以算命用tell the fortune以表示好壞皆有可能。
luck	單獨用時指一時的好運氣，但也可加負面的形容詞（如bad luck）表示倒楣。
fate	可以指發生在某人身上好或不好的命運，但是常用來表示不好的命運，前面常接有負面意義的動詞（如suffer, face, escape 等）。
destiny	強調命中注定，無法改變。
predestination	宿命論，上天決定好的人無法改變。

Unit 61 墓地

StringNet語料庫出現次數

burial	cemetery	tomb	graveyard
1031	929	875	412

burial (n.)

❖ 例句

the Bronze Age **burial** chamber

銅器時代的墓室

❖ 常用搭配詞

n. /adj. + burial

　Neanderthal, Roman, human, nearby.

burial + n.

　chamber, mound, ground, site, place, cement, rites, vault.

cemetery (n.)

❖ 例句

Arlington National **Cemetery**.

阿靈頓國家公墓

❖ 常用搭配詞

n./ adj. + cemetery

national, park, memorial, church, Catholic, city, family, state, military, royal, garden, riverside, Protestant, congressional, Christian, private, confederate, American, Muslim, communal, municipal, ancient, Presbyterian, public, historic.

tomb (n.)

❖ 例句

The treasures in the **tomb** of King Tutankhamen
圖坦卡門墳墓的寶藏

❖ 常用搭配詞

n./ adj. + tomb

chamber, family, royal, king, mummy, pharaoh, marble, emperor, cadaver, burial, stone, rock, passage, shaft.

graveyard (n.)

❖ 例句

the skeletal trees in the **graveyard**
在墓地中骸骨般的樹

❖ 常用搭配詞

 n./ adj. + graveyard

church, elephant, family, ship, royal, village, old, small, large, local, haunted, Jewish, mammoth, ancient, Chinese.

綜合整理

burial	可以指埋葬的動作、葬禮、或墓地，指墓地時特別表示考古學家發現的古代墓地，也可以在後面接名詞表示較精確的墓地說法（如 burial place和burial ground）。
cemetery	公共墓地，尤其是指一般公私立或各種宗教的墓地。
tomb	個人的墳墓，尤其是死亡的地點或場合，且多半是石棺，如埃及古墓。
graveyard	公共墓地，常指教堂旁邊的墓地，也可以指動物的墳場或廢棄物如車船的堆置場。

Unit 62 牧師

StringNet語料庫出現次數

priest	missionary	clergyman	pastor
2007	578	262	235

priest (n.)

❖ 例句

He was ordained **priest** in 1719.

他於1719年被任命為牧師。

❖ 常用搭配詞

adj. + priest

high, chief, Catholic, diocesan, secular, local, Taoist, Christian, episcopal, Franciscan, cardinal, grand.

missionary (n.)

❖ 例句

pioneer **missionary** work in Africa

在非洲的先鋒宣教工作

❖ 常用搭配詞

adj. + missionary

Christian, American, Baptist, Protestant, foreign, Catholic, Mormon, French, Spanish, Franciscan, Presbyterian, Portuguese, overseas, Islamic, Celtic, Episcopal.

clergyman (n.)

❖ 例句

His grandfather was a **clergyman**.
他的父親是神職人員。

❖ 常用搭配詞

adj. + clergyman

English, senior, Protestant, Presbyterian, Baptist, American, Catholic, Christian, Muslim.

pastor (n.)

❖ 例句

He left the army and became a Baptist **pastor**.
他離開軍隊去當浸信會的牧師。

❖ 常用搭配詞

adj. + pastor

associate, assistant, senior, local, Baptist, Protestant, Christian, Presbyterian, Pentecostal, Evangelic, reformed, American, resident.

綜合整理

priest	主要指天主教的神父，前面常接天主教相關名稱，另外也指執行儀式典禮或宗教職責的牧師，包括其他宗教。
missionary	是指派到海外宣揚基督教的傳教士。
clergyman	泛指各個宗教神職人員，尤其領導人物。
pastor	是指在固定基督教教會牧會的牧師，前面常接基督教各個派別名稱。
另外minister也表示基督教牧師，但主要的意義是政府官員中的部長。	

Unit 63 發布

StringNet語料庫出現次數

announce	issue	release
12545	7804	7717

announce (vt.)

❖ 常用句型

> **S + announce + O**
> **S + announce something to somebody**

❖ 例句

The government spokesman **announced** that the prime minister had been arrested for embezzlement.

政府發言人說總理已經因盜用公款被逮捕。

The president of the university suddenly **announced** his resignation to all the teachers.

這大學的校長突然對所有老師宣布他要辭職。

❖ 常用搭配詞

announce + (det.) _n._

  plan, retirement, intention, resignation, candidacy, decision, support, creation, name, discovery, engagement, departure, agreement, intent, change, death, result, winner, return, project, press, deal, series, production, withdrawal, partnership, purchase, appointment, arrival, merger, news, website, policy, victory, contract, opening, beginning, cancellation, establishment, dismissal, war.

(det.) _n._ + announce

government, company, band, George Bush, Microsoft, team, party, authority, police, administration, office, committee, minister, board, Johnson, department, Canada, court, China, army, president, owner, leader.

issue (vt.)

❖ 常用句型

> **S + issue + O**
> **S + issue somebody with something**
> **S + issue something to somebody**

❖ 例句

The polictian **issued** a statement denying all the news about the scandal.
這位政客發表一份聲明否認所有和此醜聞有關的新聞報導。

He **was issued with** a three-month detention order.
他收到一份為期三個月的拘留令。

The environmental policy document will **be issued** to the employees.
環保政策文件會發布給所有員工。

❖ 常用搭配詞

issue + (det.) _n._

　　statement, order, decree, report, proclamation, press, warning, license, patent, warrant, declaration, coin, series, note, apology, ruling, postage, command, currency, passport, letter, opinion.

(det.) _n._ + issue

　　government, office, court, company, committee, council, department, bank, authority, judge, army, party, Roosevelt, administration, union, emperor, church school, parliament, congress, France.

release (vt.)

❖ 常用句型

> **S + release + O**

❖ 例句

The Chinese version of this book will **be released** next month.
這本書的中文版下個月發行。

❖ 常用搭配詞

release + (det.) _n._

　　album, DVD, single, CD, term, song, record, music, video, image, game, material, recording, film, track, book, series, statement, compilation, demo, movie, information, source, work, photo, cover, picture, document, autobiography, product, list, edition, sequel, sound track, model, result.

(det.) <u>n.</u> + release

Microsoft, company, government, studio, Intel, Disney, (task) force, commodore, Japan.

綜合整理

announce	意義範圍較廣，泛指一般公布事項，強調公布，使人知道，主詞和issue以及release一樣可以大至國家，小至個人，但是發布的內容則可能是是機關團體的公務或個人的私事。
issue	是政府或機關團體或有權威的人士正式發布法令、聲明、證件或消息等，強調使之生效。
release	通常是指公布、公開、或發售音樂、文字、或影像等作品或產品，常用被動，若用主動實則主詞通常是政府、機構單位或作者；release除了表示發布，也有放棄的意思（如release all rights），使用時須小心。

Unit 64 發出

StringNet語料庫出現次數

emit	radiate	emanate
636	98	85

emit (vt.)

❖ 常用句型

> **S + emit + O**

❖ 例句

Coal plants **emit** more pollution than waste-to-energy plants.

以煤炭為能源的工廠比以垃圾作為能源的工廠排放較多的汙染物。

Some animals **emit** different alarm calls in the presence of different predators.

有些動物會針對不同掠食者發出不同的警示叫聲。

❖ 常用搭配詞

emit + n.

light, radiation, photon, electron, energy, gas, X-ray, sound, wave, pulse, beam, signal, radio, heat, smoke, stream, call, steam, vapor, noise, water, odor, warning, pollution, oxygen.

emanate (vt.)

❖ 常用句型

> **S + emanate + O**

❖ 例句

The hermit **emanates** tranquility.
這位隱士散發出平靜的氣質。

He was woken by the sound **emanating** from the boiler.
他被燒水壺發出的聲音吵醒。

❖ 常用搭配詞

<u>n.</u> + emanate(emanating) from + <u>n.</u>

sounds/ boiler, project work/ research activity, light/ theater, obnoxious odor/ the keeping of animals, authority/ people, action/ town, radiation/ the sun, music/ cubicle.

radiate (vi. / vt.)

❖ 常用句型

> **S + radiate + O**
> **S + radiate from/ out + N**

❖ 例句

The city was **rebuilt** with streets radiating from a single focal point in the center of the city.

這城市的重建是從市區的中心點開始街道呈放射狀排列。

Her face **radiated** defiance.

他的臉上流露出藐視。

❖ 常用搭配詞

n. + radiate + n.

star(sun, human being)/ energy, body(gas, bulb,)/ heat, room/ magic, he/ amazement, face/ interest, expression/ innocence.

綜合整理

emit	表示發出氣體、熱、光線、或是聲音等。
emanate	是正式用語，表示釋放氣味、光線、聲音等，也可以指散發出某種特質。
radiate	表示某物以輻射（全方位）方向釋放出光或熱，也指某人心中的感受散發出來。

Unit 65 發生

StringNet語料庫出現次數

happen	occur	take place
30861	15425	3259（BNC語料庫）

happen (vi.)

❖ 常用句型

> **S + happen**

❖ 例句

Things **happen**.

天有不測風雲。

❖ 常用搭配詞

(det.) <u>n.</u> + happen

thing, event, nothing, something, accident, incident, change, anything, everything, fact, disaster, process, attack, stuff, action, miracle, opposite, murder, crash, occurrence, story, death tragedy, massacre, battle, effect, episode, war, case, earthquake, development, phenomenon, activity, election, problem, situation, fight, coincidence.

occur (vi.)

❖ 常用句型

> **S + occur**

❖ 例句

Accidents involving drunk driving are more likely to **occur** at night.
酒駕造成的意外比較容易在晚上發生。

❖ 常用搭配詞

(det.) <u>n.</u> + occur

event, change, incident, death, accident, problem, attack, explosion, process, development, reaction, effect, war, damage, battle, error, earthquake, situation, disaster, case, phenomenon, history, eruption, riot, massacre, activity, action, growth, election, crash, fire, failure, split, injury, movement, infection, revolution, exception, collision, fighting, violence, flooding, murder, condition, flood, disease, loss, strike, shift, crisis, bombing, outbreak, rebellion, shooting, mutation, crime, story, conflict, symptom, mating, expansion, behavior, disease, cancer, headache.

take place (vi.)

❖ 常用句型

> **S + take place**

❖ 例句

Frequent exposure to natural language use creates the conditions for language acquisition to **take place**.

經常接觸自然語言使用能夠營造語言習得的環境。

❖ 常用搭配詞

(det.) <u>n.</u> + take place

event, change, activity, meeting, transaction, conversation, election, performance, interaction, session, negotiation, execution, exchange, tour, discussion, culling, concert, hunt, wedding, conference, investigation, reaction, collision, killing, incident, hearing, protest, mating, reunion, abduction, rape, carnival, selection, clinic, exhibition, festival.

綜合整理

happen	表示不在計畫中發生的事件，範圍較廣，前面可接anything/ something/ everything + 形容詞表示各種事件，也可和want一起用，表示人的意志中希望或不希望發生的事情（如I want/don't want it to happen⋯），另外也常指不好的事，如意外、災難、戰爭等。
occur	前面搭配的主詞的和happen有許多重複，但occur較正式，所以常用在新聞報導；另外occur的主詞包括人為或自然的程序中發生的現象（如strike, error, behavior, eruption, mutation, contamination），另外特別指疾病症狀的發生（如symptom, headache等）。
take place	類似中文舉行的意思，通常指一個時間延續較長的事件從頭到尾發生（如concert, exhibition, meeting等）。

Unit 66 法令

StringNet語料庫出現次數

act	statute	decree	enactment	ordinance
24556	2169	1033	310	174

act (n.)

❖ 例句

Whistleblower Protection **Act**
證人保護法案

❖ 常用搭配詞

(det.) _n._ + act

government, reform, human rights, copyright, patriot, USA Patriot, Whistleblower Protection, constitution, security, information, education, amendment, Taiwan Relation, civil marriage, sex, immigration, parliament, Faulkner, Public Health, Controlled Substance, Business Registration, Currency, Accountant, Companies, Alien Registration, Births and Deaths, Voting Rights, Endangered Species, judiciary, Corporation Taxes, espionage, terrorism, university, broadcasting, privacy, citizenship, communication, official language, tariff, drugs, navigation, surveillance, schools.

statute (n.)

❖ 例句

university **statutes** and regulations
大學法

❖ 常用搭配詞

(det.) _n._ + statute

state, Rome, Florida, university, tax, autonomy, college, federal, copyright, penalty.

decree (n.)

❖ 例句

Taiwan Education **Decree**
台灣教育法令

❖ 常用搭配詞

(det.) _n._ + decree

Royal, consent, government, emergency, council, divorce, imperial, emperor, president, educational, court.

enactment (n.)

❖ 例句

the history of legislative **enactment**
法律制定歷史

❖ 常用搭配詞

(det.) _n._ + enactment

statute law, Islamic Law, Civil Law, equality.

adj. + enactment

legislative, legal, constitutional, statutory, subsequent, congressional.

ordinance (n.)

❖ 例句

the **Ordinance** information of the City of Allen Park
Allen Park城市條例

❖ 常用搭配詞

(det.) _n._ + ordinance

city, temple, land, government, civil rights, secession, noise, town, church, preservation, crime, army, land reform, chief executive election, living wage, rent control.

綜合整理

act	指議會或國會通過的法案。
statute	是成文法，由議會或國會通過，正式寫成文件的法令；也可以指機關團體的正式法規。
decree	君王或法庭發布的法令。
enactment	泛指一般生效的法規，包括政府或民間團體制定的。
ordinance	在美國指城市鄉鎮針對居民行為規範制定的法令，也可以指或政府單位發布的法令。

Unit 67 誹謗

StringNet語料庫出現次數

libel	denigrate	slander	malign
813 (n.), 30 (v.)	132	109	54

libel (n.)

❖ 例句

The candidate sued the newspaper for **libel**.
那位候選人控告那家報社文字誹謗。

❖ 常用搭配詞

adj. + libel

　　seditious, criminal, blasphemous, alleged, famous, alleged, persistent, infamous, potential, defamatory.

libel + n.

　　suit, case, trial, action, lawsuit, claim, charge, damage.

denigrate (vt.)

❖ 常用句型

S + denigrate + O

❖ 例句

He has no intention to **denigrate** the importance of education.
他無意貶低教育的重要性。

❖ 常用搭配詞

denigrate + (det.) _n._

black, Communist, country, people, source, female, role, effort.

be denigrated by + (det.) _n._

school, musician, religion, nation, Aristotle, intelligentsia.

(det.) _n._ + denigrate

literature, website, humor, Italy, critic, statement, feminist, government.

slander (n.)

❖ 例句

The candidate sued his rival for **slander**.
那位候選人控告他的對手誹謗。

❖ 常用搭配詞

adj. + slander

political, alleged, unfounded, unqualified.

malign (vt.)

❖ 常用句型

> **S + malign + O**

❖ 例句

She was **maligned** by some of her classmates.
她被班上幾位同學中傷。

❖ 常用搭配詞

malign + (det.) _n._
  opponent, name, fighter, reputation.

(det.) _n._ + malign
  someone.

be maligned by + (det.) _n._
  historian, critic, comic, media, fan, regime, victim, enthusiast, sportscaster,
  biographer.

綜合整理

libel	是指以不實的文字或圖畫破壞別人的名譽，在語料庫中大多用作名詞，用作動詞時常是被動（如The candidate thought she had been libeled and planned to sue the newspaper.）。
slander	指捏造事實破壞別人的名譽，但是以口說言語的方式，常用作名詞。
denigrate	表示貶低、惡意詆毀，不見得有說假話，常用作動詞被動語態，（如be denigrated by intelligentsia/ other schools/ musicians），by後面的主事者多半是人或媒體等團體，句首的受事者則可以是人或非人，若用在主動則主詞和受詞可以是人或非人。
malign	表示以不實捏造事實破壞別人的名譽，但是不限於說話，也可能是文章，常用被動語態（如be maligned by/ as/ in, be maligned in the press），by後面接的主事者多半是人或媒體等團體（如be maligned by critics/ historians/ fans，少數是非人（如be maligned by the phrase），句首的受事者則可以是人或非人，很少用做主動，若用在主動則主詞和受詞可以是人或非人。

Unit 68 廢止、廢除

StringNet語料庫出現次數

abolish	repeal	annul	nullify	abrogate
1865	324	139	127	92

abolish (vt.)

❖ 常用句型

S + abolish + O

❖ 例句

When was slavery **abolished** in the US？
美國何時廢除奴隸制度？

❖ 常用搭配詞

abolish + (dnt.) _n._

slavery, death penalty, system, monarchy, council, law, office, state, institution, tax, trade, capital punishment, constitution, practice, property, school, distinction, compulsory military service, title, power, child marriage, legislature, rule, kingdom, crime, requirements, restriction.

repeal (vt.)

❖ 常用句型

S + repeal + O

❖ 例句

The law **was repealed** 50 years later.
這法條五十年後被撤銷。

❖ 常用搭配詞

repeal + n.

law, act, section, tax, amendment, legislation, prohibition, ordinance, clause, (sunset) provision, statute, portion, ban, charter.

annul (vt.)

❖ 常用句型

S + annul + O

❖ 例句

The losing candidate might seek to **annul** the election result.
落選的候選人有可能尋求使選舉結果無效。

❖ 常用搭配詞

annul the + <u>n.</u>

   elections, results, bankruptcy, effects, use.

annul + <u>n.</u>

   marriage, law, decree, treaty, result, debt, union.

nullify (vt.)

❖ 常用句型

S + nullify + O

❖ 例句

The election results **were nullified** and there would be a recount.
這場選舉結果被宣布無效，要重新計票。

❖ 常用搭配詞

nullify + (det.) <u>n.</u>

   effect, use, advantage.

abrogate (vt.)

❖ 常用句型

> **S + abrogate + O**

❖ 例句

The government announced that the treaty **had been abrogated**.
政府宣布那項協議已經取消。

❖ 常用搭配詞

abrogate + n.

   constitution, immunity, treaty, right, effect, law, agreement.

綜合整理

abolish	指正式終止某個法律或體制，尤其是已經施行多年的，如奴隸制度。
repeal	表示政府正式終止某項法律，前面的主詞和尤其是後面的受詞常是某項法條的細則條款（如act, section, provision, charter等）。
annul	常用在婚姻或法律協議。
nullify	法律用字，正式宣布某件事情無法律效力。另外也指使某件事情失去價值或效果。
abrogate	是指正式終止某項法律協議或慣例，在語料庫出現的次數不多。

Unit 69 費用

StringNet語料庫出現次數

cost	charge	fee	expenditure
26587	16240	5686	5670

expense	spending	fare	outlay
4641	3634	1387	299

cost (n.)

❖ 例句

the **cost** of living
生活費用

❖ 常用搭配詞

<u>n.</u> + cost(s)

production, construction, labor, maintenance, operating, opportunity, development, capital, transaction, fuel, energy, manufacturing, project, court, transportation, housing, health care, travel, material, transport, launch, tuition, insurance, bandwidth, equipment, building, marketing, repair, replacement, administration, service, storage, investment, product.

charge (n.)

❖ 例句

free of **charge**
免費

❖ 常用搭配詞

<u>n./ adj.</u> + charge

prescription, sewerage, local, balancing, rental, connection, community, redemption, admission, freight, handling, service, exceptional, tax, extra, initial, management, telephone, annual, water, legal, overall, transactions.

fee (n.)

❖ 例句

awyer's **fee**
律師費

❖ 常用搭配詞

<u>n./ adj.</u> + fee

license, school, legal, management, tuition, registration, entrance, entry, audit, audition, membership, transfer, fix, green, record, annual, professional, standard, court, signing-on, high, low, total, additional, appearance, cancellation, examination, lecture, crematorium, cemetery, admission, facility, consultancy, student, accommodation, cleaning, commission, consultation, training, distribution, viewing, school, rental, transaction, establishment, introduction, evaluation, affiliation, inspection, preparation, enrollment, usage, college, booking.

expenditure (n.)

❖ 例句

government **expenditure** on education
政府的教育支出

❖ 常用搭配詞

n./ adj. + expenditure

public, capital, government, total, current, national, promotional, planned, official, recurrent, projected, extra, military, political, overseas, domestic, major, potential, advertising, non-interest, single, collective, consumption, revenue, defence, consumer, development, overall, annual, service, social, tourism, family, household, university, marketing, welfare, security, state, community, investment.

expense (n.)

❖ 例句

at great **expense**
花費很大

❖ 常用搭配詞

<u>n./ adj.</u> + expense

travel, traveling, living, medical, extra, legal, business, household, funeral, out-of-pocket, removal, relocation, operating, unnecessary, running, administrative, administration, office, vast, election, public, personal, legitimate, initial, high, main, related, possible, funeral, recording, hotel, telephone, childcare, shipping, living, treatment, campaign, maintenance, interview, law, club, capital, health, clean-up, Christmas, holiday, study, house.

spending (n.)

❖ 例句

cut in military **spending**
裁減軍事開銷

❖ 常用搭配詞

<u>n./ adj</u> + spending

government, military, defence, public, consumer, capital, federal, welfare, total, current, extra, additional, high, local, health, development, education, research, real, future, Christmas, private, annual, massive, net, arms, forecasts.

fare (n.)

❖ 例句

half-**fare** for children under 120 cm
身高120公分以下的孩童半價

❖ 常用搭配詞

<u>n./ adj.</u> + fare

　bus, taxi, air, rail, railway, concessionary, train, return, full, low, high,
　standard, transport, weekend, ferry, cab, adult, hospital, plane, seafood.

outlay (n.)

❖ 例句

initial **outlay** on equpiments
最初設備支出

❖ 常用搭配詞

<u>n./ adj.</u> + outlay

　capital, initial, financial, total, modest, cash, transfer, investment,

綜合整理

cost	是指買東西、做某事、或生產產品所需支付的金錢，costs表示創辦事業的成本或房子、車子的貸款等開銷費用。
charge	是支付貨物、商品或服務的費用。
fee	是支付專業人士的費用、進入某地方的入場費、或參加某競賽活動的報名費，例如律師費是attorney fee（支付專業人士的費用）。
expenditure	是指一段時間的支出額，包含政府、機關、或個人，也可以指時間、金錢、心力的付出。
expense	範圍較廣，泛指為某件事情所花的費用，尤其是有特殊目的，如特定節日或場合，或指在工作上報支的交通費、伙食費等。
spending	政府或機構的開銷費用。
fare	是交通工具訂的票價，以及餐廳的餐飲訂價。
outlay	指創業或開辦某個活動所花的費用。

Unit 70 翻滾

StringNet語料庫出現次數

roll	toss	tumble
4665	1210	833

roll (vi. / vt.)

❖ 常用句型

> S + roll + adv.
>
> S + roll + prep. + N
>
> S + roll + somebody onto/ off something

❖ 例句

He **rolled** over on the floor, crying in pain.

他在地上翻滾，痛得哀哀叫。

The oranges **rolled** onto the sidewalk.

柳橙滾到人行道上

He **rolled** Jim into the bed gently.

他輕輕地把Jim翻轉到床上。

❖ 常用搭配詞

roll + <u>adv.</u>

up, out, over, down, back, away, around, off, along, forward, round, right, slowly, heavily, apart, together, home, sideways, gently, slightly, straight, aside, helplessly, inwards, silently, neatly, ahead, downhill, downwards, hugely.

toss (vi. / vt.)

❖ 例句

She **tossed** and turned in bed for a long time the night before the entrance examination.
聯考前一晚她在床上翻來覆去許久。

tumble (vi.)

❖ 常用句型

> **S + tumble + adv.**
> **S + tumble + prep. + N**

❖ 例句

A car was hit by the rock **tumbling** down the cliff.
有一輛轎車被從山崖滾下來的岩石擊中。

❖ 常用搭配詞

tumble + _adv._

down, out, over, back, backward, in, around, about, off, again, forward, headlong, straight, together, away, wildly, up, round.

綜合整理

roll	當不及物動詞時後面必須接副詞或介系詞，表示沿著某個表面翻滾，尤其是圓形如球等的東西，若是人的翻滾動作則是指身體平躺著滾動。
toss	toss and turn指躺在床上因睡不著而翻來覆去、不斷變換姿勢，roll over也有相同的意思或連續不規則的動作，如把生雞肉在麵粉中滾動使沾滿麵粉（to toss the chicken in flour）。此字主要的意義是指輕拋、輕擲的動作，可能是一次，如丟銅板（to toss the coin）。
tumble	是指突然往下迅速滾動，如石頭從高處滾下或雨水傾瀉而下，也指人突然摔跤。

Unit 71 翻譯

StringNet語料庫出現次數

interpretation	translation
5315	1689

interpretation (n.)

❖ 例句

He is taking an oral **interpretation** class.
他在上一門口譯課。

❖ 常用搭配詞

adj. + interpretation

 literal, restrictive, pragmatic, biblical, subjective, objective, conflicting, differing, alternative, possible, obvious, original, correct.

translation (n.)

❖ 例句

He wants a literal **translation** of this contract.
他要一份這個合約的逐字翻譯。

❖ 常用搭配詞

<u>adj.</u> + translation

　literal, simultaneous, English, Latin, German, modern, original, different.

綜合整理

interpretation	是指口頭的翻譯，另外也有解讀、詮釋行為、文藝作品的意思。
translation	包括文字和口頭的翻譯。

Unit 72 煩惱、煩躁

StringNet語料庫出現次數

obsessed	anguish	fret	brood	agonize
568	526	279	197	45

obsessed (adj.)

❖ 常用句型

> **S + be obsessed by/ with something or somebody**

❖ 例句

She is excessively **obsessed with** her weight.

她過度在乎她的體重。

❖ 常用搭配詞

be obsessed with + (one's) n.

appearance, weight, commonwealth, home, goal, research, image, work, health, progress, studies.

anguish (n.)

❖ 例句

be in **anguish**

苦惱

pain and **anguish**
痛苦

❖ 常用搭配詞

n. of anguish

cry, sense, scream, howl, moment, moan, years, groan, wail, look, feeling, gasp, quiver, emotion.

adj. + anguish

mental, personal, great, spiritual, physical, inner, real, private, psychological, silent, bitter, emotional, considerable, unspeakable, supreme, untold, national, sudden, human.

brood (vi.)

❖ 常用句型

S + brood over/ about/ on something

❖ 例句

To **brood over** life's injustice
為人生的不公平鬱鬱沉思

❖ 常用搭配詞

brood on/ over/ about + (det.) n.

loneliness, chance of survival, failure, significance, situation.

fret (vi.)

❖ 常用句型

> **S + fret (+ about/ over + N)**

❖ 例句

Don't **fret**.
不要煩惱。
He is always **fretting about** losing his job.
他總是煩惱失去他的工作。

❖ 常用搭配詞

fret about + <u> n. </u>
   possession, unemployment, way, bomb, you, performance, it, us, him.

agonize (vi.)

❖ 常用句型

> **S + agonize about/ over + N**

❖ 例句

to **agonize** over what to do
煩惱接下來要怎麼辦

❖ 常用搭配詞

agonize over/ about n.

   possession, attitude, impact, fact, world, losing one's glasses, issue, question, which route to take.

綜合整理

obsessed	通常是被動，表示過度為某人或某件事情煩惱，霸占整個心思意念以至於無法做別的事情，後面受詞之前時常是所有格（one's）。也指過度想得到某事物而心神不寧。
anguish	極度的苦惱，多半當名詞。
brood	表示一直持續不斷煩惱。
fret	常指沒有必要的煩惱，可以接事物或人作為受詞。
agonize	英式英文，表示心中掙扎要如何做決定。

Unit 73 繁榮

StringNet語料庫出現次數

flourish	thrive	prosper	boom
1012	785	478	328

flourish (vi.)

❖ 常用句型

> **S + flourish**

❖ 例句

Heavy industries **flourish** at the expense of environment conservation.
重工業繁榮興旺，犧牲了環保。

❖ 常用搭配詞

(det.) _n._ + flourish

industry, culture, business, art, trade, city, career, civilization, school, music, Christianity, town, community, literature, company, area, economy, movement, kingdom, people, empire, society, life, tradition, religion, church, style, land, crop, market, agriculture, language, crime, dynasty, idea.

boom (vi.)

❖ 常用句型

S + boom

❖ 例句

The population in the city **boomed** to 23 million in spite of the high cost of living.
縱然生活費昂貴，這個城市的人口暴增至二千三百萬。
Tourism in the country **is booming**.
這個國家的觀光業很興盛。

❖ 常用搭配詞

(det.) <u>n.</u> + boom

　population, business, industry, economy, area, town, housing, tourism,
　construction, market, sale, popularity, mine, community, trade.

thrive (vi.)

❖ 常用句型

S + thrive (+ on something)

❖ 例句

The bacterium **thrives on** warm, moist environments.
細菌容易在溫暖潮濕的環境孳生。

❖ 常用搭配詞

(det.) _n._ + thrive

industry, plant, community, business, species, city, dinosaur, company, school, bacterium, area, tree, life, animal, market, people, music, culture, world, population, civilization, race, trade, creature, forest.

prosper (vi.)

❖ 常用句型

> **S + prosper**

❖ 例句

The town **is prospering** from the results of increased tourism.

這小鎮因為觀光業增長而繁榮昌盛。

❖ 常用搭配詞

(det.) _n._ + prosper

town, business, city, company, economy, family, industry, area, community, society, firm.

綜合整理

thrive **flourish**	**thrive**和**flourish**的主詞都可以是活動、人群團體、組織、城鎮、或動植物等生物上，但thrive較flourish常用在動植物等生物上（如animal和forest），表示生長茂盛。
boom **prosper**	**boom**和**prosper**表示富裕、成功，主詞多半是有關社會經濟，例如商業、貿易、人口、地區等的名詞，很少是動植物或有關文化藝術的名詞（如literature和music等）。

Unit 74 範圍

StringNet語料庫出現次數

range	scope	confines
20118	3431	342

range (n.)

❖ 例句

a wide **range** of regional beers

一系列個地區的啤酒

❖ 常用搭配詞

range of + _n._

services, activities, possibilities, subjects, issues, topics, goods, products, people, colors, sources, interests, options, courses, facilities, sports, information, applications, factors, species, jobs, industries, skills, research, styles, books, situations, institutions, conditions, experience, environments, experience, environments, disciplines, occupations, measures, materials, matters, backgrounds, problems, opportunities, policy, views, habitats, programs, subject, contexts, media, equipment, choice, groups, customers, studies, forms, training, benefits, areas, choices, literature, documents, abilities, projects, sizes, management, languages, animals, items, credit, task, circumstances, foods, temperatures, diseases, accommodation, powers, pupils, businesses, knowledge, music, firms, prices, plants, events, resources, uses, aspects, methods, examples, teachers, disabilities, software, consumers, themes, instruments.

adj. + range of

wide, whole, full, new, broad, limited, large, vast, comprehensive, narrow, good, diverse, huge, great, complete, small, similar, different, reasonable, unique, specified, superb, restricted, considerable, varied, selected, diversified, growing, significant, valid, bewildering, maximum, defined, dazzling, sufficient, flexible, further, representative, spectacular.

v. + (det.) range of

extend, increase, broaden, limit, expand, cover, restrict, show, widen, assess, reduce, examine, see, specify, provide, indicate, describe, consider, reflect, illustrate, investigate, appreciate, represent, document, vary, explore, establish, enlarge, narrow, compare, promote.

scope (n.)

❖ 例句

to limit the **scope** of one's autobiography
限制某人自傳的範圍
There is no **scope** for questioning.
可以無限制發問。

❖ 常用搭配詞

the scope of + (det.) n.

book, chapter, work, article, paper, review, study, volume, discussion, textbook, course, section, report.

scope for + _n./ Ving_

dispute, change, cost, dissatisfaction, learning, development, choice, challenge, amendment, cost-saving, increasing, creating, raising, using, losing, reducing, making, adding, doing, extending, ensuring, improving.

_v._ + the scope

extend, limit, define, reduce, widen, broaden, expand, determine, restrict, examine, minimize.

confines (n.)

❖ 例句

The prisoner can only move within the **confines** of his ward.
囚犯只能在牢房的侷限內活動。
He is tired of the **confines** of his marriage.
他厭倦婚姻的枷鎖。

❖ 常用搭配詞

the confines of + (det.) _n._

stage, car, family, cell, classroom, community, laboratory, event time, empire, market, court, law, school, tunnel, home, Yugoslavia, Capitalism, room, prison, budget, garden, office, marriage, mortality.

_v._ + the confines of

transcend, find, leave, examine, defy, align, expand.

綜合整理

range	(1)屬於同一種類的各種不同人事物（如a wide range of subjects）可數名詞，但常用單數。(2)數量或年齡的限制範圍（如price range）可數名詞，但常用單數。
scope	不可數名詞，表示(1)某個主題、活動、或書本內容涵蓋的範圍，後面介系詞用of（如the scope of this book）。(2)某件事情發生或發展的機會，後面介系詞用for（如There is scope for further improvement.）。
confines	複數名詞，表示限制或邊界內的範圍，通常有負面意思，表示被拘束不自由，後面常接所有格+名詞，表示受制於某種不可改變的環境（如within the confines of his prison）。前面不常出現expand之類的動詞，而是出現如transcend, leave等動詞表示超越限制或離開約束。

Unit 75 反抗

StringNet語料庫出現次數

resist	rebel	revolt
3360	383	117

resist (vi. / vt.)

❖ 常用句型

> **S + resist + O**
> **S + cannot resist + (Ving) something**

❖ 例句

It's hard to **resist** the temptation of money.
很難抵抗金錢的誘惑。

He **could not resist buying** the latest iPhone.
他無法抗拒對最新iphone的購買慾。

❖ 常用搭配詞

resist + (det.) _n._

　　temptation, arrest, change, attempt, pressure, advance, effort, idea, persuasion, force, invitation, approach, dilution, attack, movement, settlement, challenge, offer, dump, designation, suggestion, move, scheme, assault, relaxation, bid, action, attacker, clamor.

rebel (vi.)

❖ 常用句型

> **S + rebel against + O**

❖ 例句

She didn't have the courage to **rebel against** her parents-in-law.
她沒有勇氣反抗她的公婆。

❖ 常用搭配詞

rebel against + (det.) <u>n.</u>

parents, master, edict, lord, husband, firm, party, command, religion, marginalization, distortion, straitjacket, commercialization, relation, domestic drudgery, values, idea, principle, female domination, vetting, command, authority figure.

revolt (vi.)

❖ 常用句型

> **S + revolt against + O**

❖ 例句

Do you have the courage to **revolt against** tyranny?
你有反抗暴政的勇氣嗎？

❖ 常用搭配詞

revolt against + (det.) <u>n.</u>

　idea, tax, rule, landlord, system, power, king.

綜合整理

resist	是指抗拒或忍受外來的誘惑、想法、或強制，包括使用武力，有拒絕配合、不受影響的意思，後面的受詞可能有正面的（例如charm, invitation）或負面的（例如pressure, temptation）意義，後面的受詞都可以是人或非人。
rebel **revolt**	**rebel**和**revolt**都是指對權威、法律、信念、或政府的反抗甚至消滅而取代政權，後面的受詞都可以是人或非人。

Unit 76 分開、分離

StringNet語料庫出現次數

separate	detach	sever	disconnect
4257	591	487	271

separate (vt.)

❖ 常用句型

> **S + separate something from/ into something**

❖ 例句

The calves were **separated from** their mother.

這些小牛和牠們的母親分開了。

He **separated** the students into four groups.

他把學生分成四組。

❖ 常用搭配詞

(det.) _n._ be separated from + (det.) _n._

the true/ the false, they/ each other, they/ one another, officers/ their families, economic autonomy/ political autonomy, passengers/ their cars, men/ women, Europeans/ Europe, calf/ mother, humankind/ the presence of God, sex-as procreation/ sex-as-fun, she/ her friends, movement/ political question, reform/ rising tide, different nations/ each other, head/ neck, larger proteins/ smaller ones, literature/ language, fact/ fantasy, cocaine base/ salt, I/ influence.

detach (vt.)

❖ 常用句型

> **S + detach something from something**
> **S + detach oneself from something/ somebody**

❖ 例句

A man **detached** himself from the crowd and moved toward the dark alley.
一位男士離開人群走進黑暗的小巷。

❖ 常用搭配詞

(det.) _n._ be detached from + (det.) _n._

carbon atom/ diamond, he/ world, label/ image, power unit/ base, line/ handle, ski/ boot, car/ train, concept/ practice, researche/ group, keyboard/ screen, community/ society, arm/ body, harbor/ town, performance/ feelings, language/ culture, mind/ body.

sever (vt.)

❖ 常用句型

> **S + sever + O**

❖ 例句

He has **severed** his links with the party.
他已經和這個團體斷絕關係。

❖ 常用搭配詞

(det.) _n._ be severed from + (det.) _n._

head/ neck, town/ church, man/ cultural roots, new plant/ parent plant, mountain/ world, he/ his spouse, cloud/ earth.

to sever one's links with + (det.) _n._

country, party, society, family, Britain, past, club.

disconnect (vt.)

❖ 常用句型

> **S + disconnect something (from something)**

❖ 例句

The burglar **disconnected** the power supply of the house.
那闖空門的竊賊切斷房子的電力。

❖ 常用搭配詞

(det.) _n._ (be) disconnected with + (det.) _n._

creatures/ each other, Mary/ her life-support machines, law/ reality, patient/ mechanical ventilator, main/ mains socket, hive/ neighbor, crampon/ boot, plate/ supply, she/ world, truck/ train, unit/ wellhead platform, people's lives/ emotional lives, people/ others.

綜合整理

separate	表示複數的人事物在空間上被分隔開來、夫妻分居、二件事物被區分給予不同對待、或某個完整的東西分解。
detach	指一樣東西離開它原本附著的東西，也可以指人心理上的疏離。
sever	為正式用語，表示物體被切斷分開、或情感關係的斷絕。
disconnect	常用在機械的分離和電力的切斷，也可指關係的斷絕或人心理上的疏離。

Unit 77 分配

StringNet語料庫出現次數

allocate	designate	allot
2527	1121	330

allocate (vt.)

❖ 常用句型

S + allocate + something to something/ somebody

❖ 例句

The government **has not allocated** sufficient resources to environmental infrastructure.

政府沒有分配足夠的資源給環保基礎建設。

Only a small portion of the State Budget **is allocated** to health care.

只有一小部分的州預算被分配給健康照護。

❖ 常用搭配詞

(num.) <u>n.</u> be allocated to + 對象/ 目的

　　fund, budget, cars, section, seats, area, tutor, studentship, money, food aid, tax, role, land, award.

be allocated + (num.) _n._

place, quota, cell, address, area, room, back-up team, number, personal secretary, patient, space, role, color, budget, seat, allowance, vote, staff, ticket, byte, observer, period.

allot (vt.)

❖ 常用句型

> **S + allot + something to something/ somebody**

❖ 例句

Each party **was allotted** 10 seats in the conference.
每個政黨在這個會議中被分配到十個席位。

❖ 常用搭配詞

(num.) _n._ be allotted to + 對象（課程名稱）

space, time, share, characteristic, trait, proportion, investment, part, task, score, point, subject,

be allotted + (num.) _n._

place, time, area, number.

designate (vt.)

❖ 常用句型

> **S + designate something as/ for something**

❖ 例句

The funds **are designated for** humanitarian aid.
這些資金是指定給人道救援。

❖ 常用搭配詞

(det.) <u>n.</u> be designated for (det.) <u>n.</u>

funds/ humanitarian aid, land/ plantation, area/ cargo, role/ him, application/ development, income/ outward giving, building/ purpose, money/ anti-pollution work, land/ industrial development, room/ activity, area/ storage of.

綜合整理

allot	常用被動語態,表示時間、金錢、空間、物品的分配,強調數量。
allocate	常用被動語態,表示依照某計畫或目的而分派人員或分配物資,強調數量或目的。
designate	常用被動語態,表示被分配做某用途,強調目的。

Unit 78 分裂

StringNet語料庫出現次數

divide	split	fracture
5937	3090	152

divide (vt.)

❖ 常用句型

> **S + divide + O**

❖ 例句

The issue of slavery **divided** the country and eventually led to civial war.
奴隸制度的議題使這國家分裂，至終引發內戰。

❖ 常用搭配詞

divide + n.

　　world, country, generation, parties, nation, society.

split (vi. / vt.)

❖ 常用句型

> **S + be split on/ over + N**
> **S + split from + N**

❖ 例句

She **split from** her husband just two months after their marriage.

她結婚二個月就和丈夫分手。

The council **is split over** the issue of health insurance.

這議會對健保的議題意見分歧。

The band has **split** up.

這樂團拆夥了。

❖ 常用搭配詞

(det.) _n._ split

　　parent, group, party, group, couple, decision, men, stack, band, plan, vote, familities.

fracture (vi. / vt.)

❖ 常用句型

> **S + fracture + O**

❖ 例句

His relationship with Maria was **fractured** by the bankruptcy of his company.
他和Maria的關係因為他公司破產而破裂。

❖ 常用搭配詞

(det.) _n._ be fractured
   relationship, talk.

綜合整理

divide	表示造成分裂，主詞不宜是人，通常是使人意見分歧的事件。在語料庫中出現次數雖然多，但是大多是表示劃分或均分的意思。
split	團體或人群因為意見不合而決裂成小群體。
fracture	國家或團體因為意見不合而決裂成不同派別。和split相似。主要的意義是表示骨折。

Unit 79 分攤、分擔

StringNet語料庫出現次數

share	apportion
11281	172

share (v.)

❖ 常用句型

> **S + share something with/ between somebody**

❖ 例句

They **share** the cost **between** them.
他們平均分攤費用。

She **shared** the water bill **with** her roommate.
他和室友分攤水費。

❖ 常用搭配詞

(det.) _n._ be shared (equally)

　　money, tasks, cost(s), housework, products, organs, profits, domestic
　　jobs, resources, decisions, income, places, fee.

apportion (vt.)

❖ 常用句型

S + apportion + O

❖ 例句

The money was equally **apportioned** among us.
我們把這筆錢平分了。

❖ 常用搭配詞

apportion + (det.) _n._

blame, remuneration, cost, money, loss, tax, punishment.

綜合整理

share	share和apportion有分擔、分攤的意思，常用被動，apportion是正式
apportion	用字，share另外還有有分享、告訴、共用等意義，在此不討論。

Unit 80 憤怒

StringNet語料庫出現次數

anger	rage	fury	indignation	wrath
3183	1183	1073	406	340

anger (n.)

❖ 例句

Her voice was trembling with **anger**.
他的聲音因憤怒而顫抖。

❖ 常用搭配詞

(V/ Ving./ Vpp) with anger

(person, voice) tremble, react, express, (eyes) harden, burn, flush, (hands, voice, person) shake, talk, (tongue) loosen, fume, (knee) twitch, do, (face) darkened, sob, stiffen, quiver, blaze, seethe, weep, flash, tinge, explode, spark, greet, ask, think, light, scream, (eyes) glitter, (eyes) flare, (blood, person) boil, redden, (eyes) blaze, (face) contort, overwhelm, fall, howl, (eyes, person) sparkle, bristle, (chest) shrivel, (face) suffuse, say, (eyes) alight, smolder, respond, (face) distort, erupt, (face) twist, whoop, (face) cloud.

a (n) + _n._ of anger

shiver, expression, explosion, state, edge, outburst, mixture, fit, mood, feeling, hint, flare, look, degree, flame, display, seething, sense, build-up, flash, spiral, occurrence, wail, mask, fist, tinge, howl, act, flick, spurt, surge, wave, blaze, package, frenzy, flush, note, glare, combination, tide, stab, cry, screech, thread, stir.

rage (n.)

❖ 例句

He tend to stammers when he is in a **rage**.
他一生氣說話就會結結巴巴。

❖ 常用搭配詞

<u>V/ Ving./ Vpp</u> with rage

bristle, roar, (face, feature) contort, weep, explode, choke, flush, boil, incense, consume, (face) stamp, cry, shake, seethe, spit, (face) distort, splutter, (eye) glitter, (face) work, (face) lean, (face) suffuse, tremble, howl, cream, (face) darken, smolder, sob, blind, fume.

a (n) + <u>n.</u> of rage

cry, roar, yelp, Lamentation, scream, howl, burst, flash, access, pitch, storm, avalanche, tide, bellow, surge, mixture, wave, show, mask, combination, frenzy, shriek, yell, snarl, fit.

fury (n.)

❖ 例句

His eyes blazed with **fury**.
他的眼神閃著怒火。

❖ 常用搭配詞

<u>V/ Ving./ Vpp</u> with fury

(face) contort, react, consume, (mouth) twist, snort, burst, shudder, (eye) glitter, quiver, fizzle, roar, quiver, shake, (mouth) compress, (eye) blaze, charge, squawking, seethe, glow, burn, explode, (face) redden, (figure) shake, jump, boil, greet.

a (n) + <u>n.</u> of fury

tongue, avalanche, moment, explosion, pitch, flood, surge, rush, parody, look, gesture, face, growl, mask, crescendo.

indignation (n.)

❖ 例句

Fueled by righteous **indignation**, hundreds of thousands of people participated in the protest.
數十萬人義憤填膺地參加這場示威抗議。

❖ 常用搭配詞

<u>V/ Ving./ Vpp</u> with indignation

(voice) quiver, (eyebrow) arch, tremble, smolder, flush, (chest) puff, bristle, snort, heave, blush, boil, splutter, fume, seethe, flush, shudder, shiver, recoil, rise, suffuse, burn, (eye) blaze, retort, (eye) widen, respond, reject, fizz, (eye) glint, (voice) quiver.

a + _n._ of indignation

storm, burst, state, yelp, pitch, fervor, show, hint, flash, rush.

wrath (n.)

❖ 例句

The President's statement incurred the **wrath** of the common people.
總統的言論引起大眾的憤怒。

❖ 常用搭配詞

_v._ the wrath of

draw, fear, incur, mitigate, provoke, risk, bring, get, arouse, attract, escape, face, avoid, dare, include, appease, endure, awaken, spark, feel.

綜合整理

anger	泛指一般怒氣。
rage	和fury一樣表示無法控制的怒氣。
fury	表示無法控制的怒氣。
indignation	是指因感覺受到侮辱或不公平對待而產生的震驚憤怒。
wrath	是正式用字，表示極度憤怒。

Unit 81 奮鬥、奮力

StringNet語料庫出現次數

fight	struggle	strain	strive
10377	3590	1243	1000

fight (vi)

❖ 常用句型

> **S + fight (+ prep. + N)**

❖ 例句

People **fight** for freedom.

人們會爭取自由。

❖ 常用搭配詞

fight for + (det.) _n._

control, breath, life, survival, air, compensation, freedom, justice, king, supremacy, independence, possession, Britain, power, space, market, improvements, peace, word, liberty, jobs, business, attention, custody, calm, territory, women, democracy, secession, money, reform, dignity.

fight against + (det.) _n._

injustice, racism, wage reduction, sensation, prejudice, need, impulse, instinct, HIV, Capitalism, government, stereotype, drought, lack, recession, doubt, evil, threat.

fight to + _v._

keep, get, save, control, defend, hold, preserve, retain, make, prevent, protect, stay, have, regain, maintain, win.

struggle (vi.)

❖ 常用句型

> **S + struggle (+ prep. + N)**
> **S + struggle to + Vroot**

❖ 例句

She **was struggling** to survive in the company.
她掙扎著在那家公司生存。

❖ 常用搭配詞

struggle for + (det.) _n._

power, existence, survival, independence, control, democracy, justice, freedom, life, recognition, health, women's rights, supremacy, peace, equality, influence, dominance, liberation, dignity, promotion, socialism, resources, world, unification, reforms, mastery, admission, territory, air, education, ownership, jurisdiction, liberty.

struggle to _v._

get, keep, find, make, survive, maintain, cope, control, hold, overcome, free, stay, come, retain, bring, contain, understand, put, do, pay, break, escape, achieve, recover, meet, remember, establish, reach, rise, avoid, regain, match, score, think, take, learn, fill, follow, preserve, create, express, open, live, breathe, hide, balance, stop, give, adapt, reconcile, suppress, emerge, raise, master, provide, catch, complete, produce, beat, reassert, start, deal, impose, remain, turn, help, work, fulfil, adjust, prove, change, save, ensure, repay, gain, manage.

strain (vi.)

❖ 常用句型

S + strain + to Vroot
S + strain + for something

❖ 例句

I **strained** to hear my teacher's every word in the noisy restaurant.
在那吵雜的餐廳我努力地想聽到我老師說的每一個字。

❖ 常用搭配詞

strain for + (det.) _n._

progression, breakthrough, outlet, breath, approval, happiness.

strain to + _v._

hear, see, catch, get, make, finish, reach, gain, keep, read, hold, break, start, listen, remember, pull, look, find, force, stay, follow, say, conjure, have, discern, contain, build, propel, identify.

strive (vi.)

❖ 常用句型

> **S + strive + to Vroot**
> **S + strive for/ after something**

❖ 例句

Her father asked her to **strive for** perfection in her school work.
她父親要求她在課業上力求完美。

❖ 常用搭配詞

strive for + (det.) <u>n.</u>

excellence, perfection, success, peace, calm, freedom, control, influence, authority, goodness, recognition, justice, immortality, progress, sobriety, power, survival.

strive to + <u>v.</u>

keep, achieve, make, improve, get, find, maintain, do, create, ensure, sustain, provide, become, overcome, build, bring, avoid, put, raise, live, emulate, protect, see, reduce, fulfil, increase, gain, meet, control, give, remain, acquire, promote, establish, calm, present, balance, express, please, develop, analyze, move, understand, address, show, contain, serve, accelerate, produce, relax, catch, uphold, undermine, release, apply, eliminate, change.

綜合整理

fight	指努力嘗試以達成某事或得到某物。也可接against表示奮力對抗。
struggle	強調經過千辛萬苦，排除萬難的奮鬥。
strain	strain常指身體體力上的奮力完成某動作，不常用作動詞，在語料庫的數量多是名詞，而且因為用法多而解釋不同。
strive	strive表示努力奮鬥，但是和前面其他動詞不同的地方是它可以用來表示個人力爭上游以達到更美好的境界，所以受詞可接perfection和excellence等字。

Unit 82 方法

StringNet語料庫出現次數

way	method	approach	means	measure	methodology
109753	17275	16879	12599	11059	1023

way (n.)

❖ 例句

He asked his coach for a more efficient **way** of hitting a golf ball.

他要求教練教他更有效率打高爾夫球的方法。

The counselor showed the children that there are many **ways** of showing love other than sex.

這位輔導老師教導這些小孩除了性行為以外還有許多其他表達愛的方式。

❖ 常用搭配詞

adj. + way

extreme, effective, traditional, further, odd, common, easy, decisive, various, simple, convenient, possible, unique, efficient, same, best, usual, natural, popular, practical, American, general, specific, appropriate, primary, innovative, straightforward, basic, equivalent, clever, fundamental, precise, accurate, legal, valid.

means (n.)

❖ 例句

This task is by no **means** as simple as they expected.
這個工作絕對不像他們預期的那麼簡單。

The candidate gave support to homosexual groups as a **means** of soliciting votes.
這位候選人支持同性戀做為吸引選票的手段。

❖ 常用搭配詞

means of + <u>n./ ving</u>

transport, emergency communication, avoiding litigation, rewarding personal bravery, sending message, hiding from, identification, escape, expression, propagation, promoting discussion, economic diversification, expanding audience, impressing visitors, raising money, combating communism.

method (n.)

❖ 例句

There have been several innovative treatment **methods** for cancers.
現在已經有幾種治療癌症的新方法。

The primary school principal likes the teachers to experiment on various teaching **methods** to cater to different learning styles.
這小學校長喜歡老師實驗各種教學法以配合不同的學習風格。

❖ 常用搭配詞

n. + method

teaching, research, production, construction, training, input, control, voting, assessment, design, treatment, analysis, business, compression, testing, payment, communication.

approach (n.)

❖ 例句

The unorthodox **approach** of teaching English grammar seems to work well for his students.

這種非正統的英文文法教學方式似乎對這些學生滿有用。

The scholar adopted an empirical **approach** to interpret the theory.

這學者採用實證的方法來解釋這個理論。

❖ 常用搭配詞

n. + approach

landing, top-down, design, management, landing, novel, development, marketing, team, treatment, engineering, evaluation, learning, research, teaching, business, comparison, step-by-step.

measure (n.)

❖ 例句

New safety **measures** are being taken in airports after the terrorist attack.
在恐怖攻擊以後機場實施新的安全措施。

The newborn baby was kept in an incubator as a precautionary **measure**.
新生兒被放在保溫箱做為預防措施。

❖ 常用搭配詞

n. + measure

　security, safety, ballot, control, emergency, protection, reform, enforcement.

adj. + measure

　temporary, desperate, precautionary, extreme, preventive, drastic, defensive, repressive, protective, harsh, cost-saving, last, severe, corrective, remedial, controversial, aggressive.

methodology (n.)

❖ 例句

The teacher has been developing a new **methodology** for assessing language proficiency.
這位老師研發出一種新的評估語言能力的方法。

He is taking a course on research **methodologies**.
他在修研究方法課程。

❖ 常用搭配詞

(det.) <u>n.</u> + methodology

design, development, research, teaching, programming, testing, engineering, management, evaluation, experiment, modeling, assessment, retrieval.

綜合整理

way	意義最廣，泛指達成某件事情所使用的方法，一般用字，少用在專業領域，常用句型有 adj. + way of + Ving（例如 the easiest way of solving the problem, effective way of doing this, etc.）。
means	和way意義相近，表示做事或達成某件事情的方法，有可能是行動、物件、工具或系統。常用句型有by no means及as a means of + Ving，前面可接負面意義的形容詞如illegal, unfair, unlawful等。
method	表示做某件事情為大眾所知道或使用的有計劃性的方法，前面常接專業名詞如教學（teaching）、建築（construction）、或醫療（treatment）等。
approach	意指做事或解決某問題或狀況的想法或行動，不如method有計畫性和組織性。
measure	常用複數，表示解決問題的行動，可指官方或公務上的權宜之計或緊急措施，所以會接drastic, tough, desperate, extreme等形容緊急措施的形容詞。
methodology	則是指做研究或某種工作的一套方法或原則，可包括數個methods。

Unit 83 防止、妨礙、阻止

StringNet語料庫出現次數

prevent	block	inhibit	prohibit	frustrate
10406	2571	1203	1021	626

hinder	hamper	obstruct	impede
593	528	409	361

prevent (vt.)

❖ 常用句型

> **S + prevent something/ somebody from doing something**

❖ 例句

The teacher tried to **prevent** the group discussion from becoming dominated by just one or two students.

老師試著避免小組的討論被少數一、二位同學獨佔。

❖ 常用搭配詞

prevent + N from + _Ving_

   taking, becoming, doing, going, getting, having, making, seeing, working, giving, reaching, entering, turning, continuing, drying, acting, falling, attending, leaving, saying, using, pulling, moving, playing, thinking, selling, keeping, feeling, recognizing,, winning, coming, joining, forming, running, occurring, slipping, enforcing, acquiring, spreading, carrying, developing, finding, bending, repeating, dealing, blowing, relying, firing, rising, reducing, cheating, publishing, producing, convening, claiming, disposing, gripping, reviewing, crushing, engaging, touring.

to prevent + (det.) _n._ from Ving

defendant tenant, government, police, press, company, glider, patient, parties, crown, horse, child, dog, machine, skin, group, marcher, court, director, animal, reaction, employee, mixture, plaintiff, assembly, landlord, team, house, defence, expert, sun, seller, public, body, offender, institute, country, industry, female, paint, disk, magnet, American, royalist, fact, inflow, bud, dissenter.

block (vt.)

❖ 常用句型

> **S + block + O**

❖ 例句

The government **blocked** the import of Australian agricultural products.
這政府封鎖澳洲農產品的進口。

❖ 常用搭配詞

to block (det.) _n._ (of)

road, way, flow, induction, absorption, release, passage, reappointment, center, import, action, enforcement, dumping, production, enhancement, city, issue, renewal, removal, spread, movement, picture, proliferation, appointment, effect, replication, formation, suppression, path, line, gift, cluster, route.

be blocked by + (det.) _n._

city, imposition, monopolies, antagonists.

inhibit (vt.)

❖ 常用句型

> **S + inhibit + O**
> **S + inhibit somebody from doing something**

❖ 例句

Recording the interview may **inhibit** the interviewees from expressing their real views.

在面談時錄影可能會使受訪者不敢表達真正的看法。

❖ 常用搭配詞

be inhibited by + (det.) + _n._

amiloride, presence, need, existence, fact, body, protein, heparin, antibodies, dids, indomethacin.

inhibit + (det.) _n._

development, growth, absorption, release, formation, application, ability, action.

prohibit (vt.)

❖ 常用句型

> **S + prohibit somebody from doing something**

❖ 例句

His physical problem **prohibits** him from entering regular school.
他的身體問題使他無法就讀一般學校。

frustrate (vt.)

❖ 常用句型

> **S + frustrate + O**

❖ 例句

The environmental program was **frustrated** by the increasing amount of pollution coming from the neighboring areas.
鄰近地區帶來的汙染使這個環保計畫受挫。

❖ 常用搭配詞

frustrate + (det.) _n._
    purpose, wish, aims, intention, attempt, object, monitoring, flow, goal.

be frustrated by (det.) + _n._

  lack, confnes, failure, restrictions, opposition, circumstances.

hamper (vt.)

❖ 常用句型

> **S + hamper + O**

❖ 例句

His research plan **was hampered** by shortage of funds.
他的研究計畫因為資金不足而受阻。

❖ 常用搭配詞

be hampered by + (det.) _n._

  fact, lack, injury, absence, Harrison (person), differences, shortage, emotion, obstacle, branagh, midnight, obstruction, fear, poll, staff, uncertainties, presence, reluctance, influence, gun, thought, inability, domination, illness, slowness, need, existence, beating, discovery.

(det.) _n._ be hampered

  operation, college, progress, countries, efforts, studies, body, corpora, England, mobility, process, move, research, force, precaution, education, rundown, judge, recovery, conservation, review, diplomacy, investigation.

hinder (vt.)

❖ 常用句型

S + hinder + O

❖ 例句

Malnutrition may **hinder** children's learning.
營養不良會造成兒童學習遲緩。

❖ 常用搭配詞

to hinder + (det.) _n._ (of)

development, process, achievement, work, growth, progress, implementation, ball, advancement, setting, establishment, diffusion, return, exchange, child, study, cause, absorption, fight, creation.

obstruct (vt.)

❖ 常用句型

S + obstruct + O

❖ 例句

They were fined for **obstructing** the police.
他們因妨礙警務執行被罰鍰。

❖ 常用搭配詞

to obstruct + (det.) _n._

  police, activity.

impede (vt.)

❖ 常用句型

> **S + impede + O**

❖ 例句

The unrest **impeded** the development of the tourism in the country.

這國家的動盪不安阻礙了他們觀光業的發展。

❖ 常用搭配詞

to impede + (det.) _n._ (of)

  development, course, process, functioning, expansion, recovery, passage, view, collection, blood, transition, work, flow, peace, force, nationalist, supply, transit, deployment, growth, sight, infiltration, market, working, divulgation, implementation, agency, application, reduction, music.

(det.) _n._ + impede

  way, condition, factor, iron, restriction, narrative, danger, wall, Cairo, recruitment, weather, rule, council, girl, arm, movements, area, need, turn, current, pressure, difficulty, contour, progress, defendant, desire, forces, water, weakness, school, ambiguity, climate, claim.

綜合整理

prevent	prevent表示使某件事情無法或不可能發生，和片語keep… from…和 stop…from…意思相同。
block	阻止某件事情發生、發展、或成功。也指擋住去路以阻止前進。意思和obstruct相似。
inhibit	表示使一件已經開始的事情或過程很困難而不能順利進展，常用在生物學上，常用被動語態。還表示使人不好意思或擔心而不敢暢所欲言（例如Recording the interview may inhibit the interviewees from expressing their real views.）。
prohibit	prohibit大多表示禁止的意思，表示阻止的意思時是正式用字，亦即使某件事情無法或不可能發生，在語料庫的句子絕大多數是表示禁止的意思，因此在此不提供搭配詞例子。
frustrate	frustrate指的是使人的計畫、意圖、辛勞等無法成功。
hinder	表示使一件已經開始的事情或過程很困難而不能順利進展。
hamper	表示使一件已經開始的事情或過程很困難而不能順利進展，常用在被動句。
obstruct	意思和block相似，表示使某件事情無法發生，和prevent、prohibit一樣（例如obstruct the police 妨礙警務執行）。
impede	表示使一件已經開始的事情或過程很困難而不能順利進展。
注意prevent和inhibit的差別：在句子The law is intended to prevent crime.其中 prevent不能替換為inhibit，意思是杜絕犯罪的發生，而不是使犯罪進展困難。	

Unit 84 豐富的

StringNet語料庫出現次數

rich	abundant	plentiful	copious
7622	594	410	181

rich (adj.)

❖ 例句

The patient needs foods **rich** in Vitamin A.

那位病人需要富含維他命A的食物。

❖ 常用搭配詞

rich in + <u>n.</u>

species, mineral, wildlife, fiber, vitamin calcium, iron, protein, nitrogen, oxygen, wool, flavor, plant, gold, fat, magnesium, carbohydrate, forest, animal, oil, imagery, melody, character, yeast, food, possibility, culture, tradition, diversity, beauty, detail, symbolism.

abundant (adj.)

❖ 例句

Caterpillars provide **abundant** protein for birds.
毛毛蟲提供鳥類豐富的蛋白質。

❖ 常用搭配詞

abundant + (det.) _n._

evidence, supply, life, water, harvest, species, supplies, remains, wildlife, food, material, hair, use, source, flower, rainfall, information, rain, plant, mineral, documentation, element, nitrogen, opportunity, fossil, tear, potential, fuel, protein, fish, crop, example, energy, gas.

plentiful (adj.)

❖ 例句

The college student enjoyed a **plentiful** supply of money from his parents.
這大學生的父母給他充分的金錢。

❖ 常用搭配詞

plentiful + _n._

supply, evidence, labor, food, water, harvest, hay, fuel, diet, opportunity, resource.

(det.) _n._ be plentiful

food, labor, money, water, equipment, fish, job, material.

copious (adj.)

❖ 例句

Wash the wound with **copious** amounts of water.
用大量的水沖洗這個傷口。

❖ 常用搭配詞

copious + (det.) <u>n.</u>

amount, note, quantity, thirst, evidence, reference, salivation, saliva, literature, supply, mucus, information, material, source, illustration, documentation, data, color, nectar, use, record, expectoration, sweat, diarrhea.

綜合整理

rich	雖然在語料庫出現次數高，但多半表示有錢的意思，表示豐富時多用在片語rich in，富含某物質，尤其是營養素。
abundant	數量超過足夠，前面可接最高級the most，後面常接source of + n.或supply of + n.。
plentiful	數量超過足夠，常用作主詞補語修飾名詞主詞（例如Wine is cheap and plentiful in the country.），後面最常接supply of + n.（例如a plentiful supply of food）。
copious	後最常接amounts of + n.，也常用在醫學上，接人體排出的物質（如mucus, sweat, saliva等）。

Unit 85 服裝

StringNet語料庫出現次數

clothes	dress	clothing	garment	apparel
6864	4479	2065	1256	66

clothes (n.)

❖ 例句

He prefers to wear casual **clothes**.
他偏好穿便服。

❖ 常用搭配詞

adj. + clothes

　scruffy, clerical, peculiar, tight, dark, Australian, plain, fashionable, bright, immaculate, threadbare, funny, bright-colored, casual, elegant, sensual.

dress (n.)

❖ 例句

Does the restaurant have a **dress** code?
到這餐廳用餐有服裝規定嗎？

❖ 常用搭配詞

adj./ n. + dress

wedding, evening, silk, cotton, summer, satin, party, cocktail, court, velvet, taffeta, print, linen, lace, morning, day, muslin, casual, distinctive, ceremonial, low-cut, fashionable, elegant, revealing, elaborate, female, tartan, academic, ethnic, gold, maternity, wool, designer, afternoon, chiffon tennis, bridesmaid, Sunday, mourning, ballet, dancing, school, walking-out, graduation, fancy, travelling.

clothing (n.)

❖ 例句

Most of her salary is spent on food and **clothing**.
她的薪資大部分花在食物和服裝。

❖ 常用搭配詞

pos. + clothing

women's, men's, child's, wolf's, sheep's.

adj. + clothing

contemporary, protective, outdoor, thick, expensive, white, male, plain, Turkish, fashionable, everyday, warm, suitable, poor, light, dark, tight, waterproof, inadequate.

garment (n.)

❖ 例句

The **garment** manufacturing industry in this country is accelerating.
這個國家的服裝製造業快速發展。

❖ 常用搭配詞

adj. + garment

knitted, outer, woolen, upper, new, white, finished, other, black, old, particular, strange, suitable, completed, single, cheap, offending, whole, heavy, simple, little, flimsy, plain, similar, complete, Islamic, perfect, interesting, ideal, bridal, protective, striped, national, special, ecclesiastical, various, actual, elaborate, functional, appropriate, basic, masculine, gorgeous, voluminous, shapeless, fitting, frilly, dark, original, infested, Chinese, athletic, sporting, hard-wearing.

apparel (n.)

❖ 例句

He adorned his beautiful wife with fine **apparel**.
他給他的美麗妻子穿精美的服裝。

❖ 常用搭配詞

adj. + apparel

fine, protective, fancy, female, decent, working, canine, Scottish, tennis, designer, textile, fashion.

綜合整理

clothes	複數，指一件一件的衣服。
dress	可指女性洋裝或男女特殊類型或特殊場合穿的衣服（如evening gown）。
clothing	是單數，表示衣物的總稱，範圍廣泛。
garment	正式用字，可數名詞，用在服裝產業（如garment industry, garment business等）。
apparel	不可數名詞，表示外衣，裝飾，可用在動物服裝及植物的外覆。

Unit 86 福利

StringNet語料庫出現次數

benefit	welfare	perk
15005	4753	270

benefit (n.)

❖ 例句

He received unemployment **benefit** after losing his job.
他失業後領失業救濟金。

❖ 常用搭配詞

<u>n.</u> + benefit

state, child, fringe, sickness, invalidity, housing, welfare, money, employee, consumer, insurance, family, car, cash, maternity, shareholder, tax, pension.

welfare (n.)

❖ 例句

There are many impoverished families living on **welfare** in this area.
這一地區有許多領救濟金的貧困家庭。

❖ 常用搭配詞

<u>n.</u> + welfare

animal, child, family, state, education, community, infant, student, court, government, boys, tax, maternity, staff, insurance, company, group, nursery, material, employee, equilibrium, factory, youth, consumer, miner, world, county, housing, population, shareholder, unemployment, pension, employer.

perk (n.)

❖ 例句

One of the **perks** of this job is free parking in the basement of this building.
這份工作的津貼之一是在本棟地下停車場免費停車。

❖ 常用搭配詞

perks of + (det.) <u>n.</u>

job, office, church, manor, crew, premiership, incumbency.

綜合整理

benefit	意義範圍較廣，可指在工作上或保險所得到的金錢或好處。（fringe benefit是指公司給予一般員工薪水以外的正常福利，包括退休金，健保等），在英式英語中則是指表示政府給予失業、貧病等有需要的人民的金錢。
welfare	表示政府給予失業、貧病等有需要的人民的金錢，相當於英式英語中的benefit（美式= on welfare，英式= benefit）。
perk	是正式用字，常用複數，指總統或公司高階幹部或表現優異職員的福利，包含自用車、高爾夫球等。

Unit 87 符合

StringNet語料庫出現次數

meet	satisfy	conform	tally	fulfill
32821	2811	1218	105	64

meet (vt.)

❖ 常用句型

> **S + meet + O**

❖ 例句

The outcome does not **meet** their expectation.
結果不如他們預期。

❖ 常用搭配詞

meet + (det.) <u>n.</u>

needs, requirement, demand, challenge, criteria, standard, target, deadline, term, objective, expectation, obligation, wish, commitment.

satisfy (vt.)

❖ 常用句型

> **S + satisfy + O**

❖ 例句

None of the applicants **satisfied** their requirements.
沒有一個應徵者符合他們的條件。

❖ 常用搭配詞

satisfy + (det.) <u>n.</u>

requirement, need, demand, condition, criteria, expectation, term, wish, principle, judgment, standard, quality, rule, purpose, regulation,

conform (vi.)

❖ 常用句型

> **S + conform to/ with + N**

❖ 例句

She does not **conform** to the stereotype of a school teacher.
她不符合一個學校老師的傳統形象。

❖ 常用搭配詞

conform to + (det.) <u>n.</u>

demand, rule, convention, requirement, principle, idea, expectation, wish, need, picture, commandment, custom, value, goal, condition, observation, standard.

tally (vi.)

❖ 常用句型

> **S + tally (+ with + N)**

❖ 例句

The data in his paper do not **tally with** the data obtained from the experiment.
他報告上的數據和實驗結果的數據不符合。

❖ 常用搭配詞

tally with + (det.) <u>n.</u>

number, figure, requirement.

fulfill (vt.)

❖ 常用句型

> **S + fulfill + O**

❖ 例句

He is trying to **fulfill** his role as a father.
他在試著做好父親的角色。

❖ 常用搭配詞

fulfill + (det.) <u>n.</u>

function, requirement, role, demand, wish, purpose, order, commitment, task, will, demand, need.

綜合整理

meet	指做到別人所要求、需要、或預期的事情，主詞非人，後面最常接 needs。
satisfy	指符合要求或標準等，主詞可以是人或非人。
conform	指符合大眾的預期或想法，主詞可以是人或非人。
tally	tally with 常和數字或言論有關，表示完全吻合，主詞非人（例如 requirement, figure, data, theory, measurement等）。
fulfill	表示做到必須的角色、承諾或功能等，也常表示實現（如fulfill one's promise），主詞可以是人或非人。

Unit 88 符號

StringNet語料庫出現次數

character	mark	sign	symbol
12249	11846	10187	3011

character (n.)

❖ 例句

It is difficult for most foreigners to learn to read Chinese **characters**.
大部分外國人很難學會閱讀中文字。

❖ 常用搭配詞

n. + character
  ascii.

adj. + character
  alphanumeric, printable, shadier, optical, architectural, Greek, Chinese.

mark (n.)

❖ 例句

Chinese language has different quotation **marks** from English language.
中文的引號和英文的引號不同。

❖ 常用搭配詞

<u>n.</u> + mark

exclamation, metronome, punctuation, quotation, batsman, stretch, trade, chalk, question, exam, brand, identification, assessment.

<u>adj.</u> + mark

fair-trade, high-water, distinguishing, identifying, halfway.

sign (n.)

❖ 例句

He didn't see the warning **sign** and fell into the pit.
他沒看到警告標誌因而掉進洞裡。

❖ 常用搭配詞

<u>n.</u> + sign

dollar, warning, neon, plus, minus, stop, traffic, star, thumb up, for sale, danger, call, advertising, shop, street, entry, direction.

<u>adj.</u> + sign

tell-tale, linguistic.

symbol (n.)

❖ 例句

Fe is the chemical **symbol** for iron.
Fe 是鐵的化學符號。

❖ 常用搭配詞

n. + symbol

　fertility, language.

adj. + symbol

　phonetic, referential, phallic, mathematical, religious, Christian, political,
national.

綜合整理

mark	常用來指標點符號、商標等，也泛指手寫或印出來的形狀或符號等。
character	含有多重意義，大多指戲劇中的人物，表示符號時是指用在書寫、印刷、或電腦上的文字、記號等。在語料庫出現的次數雖多，但包含其他多種不同的意義。
sign	泛指有特殊涵意的圖畫或形狀。
symbol	是有特殊涵意或代表某種組織或思想理念的圖畫或形狀，也指代表聲音、數量、或化學元素的字母、數字、或標誌。

Unit 89 腐爛、腐朽

StringNet語料庫出現次數

rotten	decay	decompose	putrid	moulder
756	386	135	50	21

rotten (adj.)

❖ 例句

Bananas go **rotten** quickly.
香蕉腐爛得很快。

❖ 常用搭配詞

rotten + <u>n.</u>
　apple, egg, plum, orange, smell, potato.

decay (vi.)

❖ 常用句型

> **S + decay**

❖ 例句

The body has already **decayed** when found.
那屍體被發現時已經腐爛。

❖ 常用搭配詞

decayed + _n._

    wood, timber, animal, tree, teeth, body, remnant, fence, waterwheel, house, environment, head, masses, vegetation, plant, food, material, branch, furnishings, twig.

(det.) _n._ + decay

    wood, bone, organ, building.

decompose (vi.)

❖ 常用句型

> **S + decompose**

❖ 例句

Do the garbage bags **decompose**?

這些垃圾袋會分解嗎？

❖ 常用搭配詞

(det.) _n._ + decompose

    sample, root, body, forest, environment, snail.

decomposed + _n._

    body, remains, cheese, poultry, head, skeleton, snail, forearm, wood, form, debris, granite, piece.

putrid (adj.)

❖ 例句

There is a **putrid** smell in the cave.
洞穴裡有股惡臭的味道。

❖ 常用搭配詞

putrid + _n._

　smell, breath, stench, meat, flesh, odor, liver, taste, rottenness.

moulder (vi.)

❖ 常用句型

> **S + moulder**

❖ 例句

The dead soldiers' bodies lay **mouldering** in the battle field.
陣亡的軍人屍體遺留在戰場上腐爛。

❖ 常用搭配詞

(det.) _n._ + molder

　man, beast, fabric, wall, trousers, body, prison.

綜合整理

rotten	表示自然的化學變化造成的腐爛，後面常接食物，如雞蛋或水果等。也形容事物（例如a rotten idea =爛主意），表示很爛。
decay	表示自然的化學變化造成的腐爛，後面接的名詞可以是動植物或物品，但不能是人。
decompose	比較常表示生物或分子等的分解。
putrid	表示死亡動植物的腐臭，常用來形容腐臭味，後面時常接表示氣味的名詞或肉類，另外也表示令人不悅的。
moulder	表示腐朽，主詞可以是人、動物、衣物、或物品，也常以分詞片語形式接在名詞後面。

Unit 90 輔助、援助

StringNet語料庫出現次數

help	aid	assistance
10672	9268	4290

help (n.)

❖ 片語

with the **help** of something/somebody
有某事物或某人的幫助
a cry for **help**
呼求幫助

❖ 常用搭配詞

adj. + help

　practical, professional, further, financial, legal, general, sympathetic, necessary, full, adequate, confidential, generous, personal, friendly.

aid (n.)

❖ 片語

legal **aid** system
法律扶助制度
something as an **aid** to
以某物做為輔助

to come to one's **aid**
來幫忙某人

❖ 常用搭配詞

adj. + aid

legal, military, economic, financial, humanitarian, Christian, foreign, medical, useful, important, federal, valuable, regional, mutual, suspended, powerful, substantial, international, British, additional, visual, direct, bilateral, increased, massive, environmental, official, technical, practical, unconditional, overseas, generous, specific, diagnostic, optical, extra, anti-drug.

n. + aid

grant, emergency, food, hearing, development, US, action, famine, government.

assistance (n.)

❖ 例句

legal advice and **assistance**
法律諮詢與協助
with the **assistance** of something/somebody
有某事物或某人的幫助

❖ 常用搭配詞

adj. + assistance

financial, technical, military, economic, mutual, humanitarian, legal, practical, valuable, selective, considerable, substantial, American, direct, medical, technological, international.

n. + assistance

relocation, emergency, US, research, unemployment.

綜合整理

help	help指的幫助主導性較強，而aid和assistance 指的是從旁協助。Help當名詞時前面不常放形容詞或名詞，而是放所有格較多，表示來自某人的幫助。
aid	指政府或機構提供的金錢或物資的救助（如grant aid, foreign aid）、幫助完成某事的協助或建議（legal aid, technical aid）、以及輔助工具（如hearing aid, visual aid），最常出現在前面的形容詞是legal (legal aid)。
assistance	泛指協助支援，但不包含建議的部分（例如常用在片語advice and assistance），也不包含工具，最常出現在前面的形容詞是financial （financial assistance）。

Unit 91 富有、富裕

StringNet語料庫出現次數

rich	wealthy	prosperous	affluent	well-off	opulent
7622	1529	682	384	128	120

rich (adj.)

❖ 片語

an area rich in something
富含某物的地區
to strike it rich
發橫財
the gap between rich and poor
貧富差距

❖ 常用搭配詞

rich + n.

man, peasant, source, variety, vein, mixture, country, seam, woman, harvest, merchant, diversity, family, fund, soil, reward, sauce, widow, crop, prize, habitat, sea, future, architecture, area.

wealthy (adj.)

❖ 片語

the offspring of the wealthy
有錢人家的後代
extremely wealthy
家財萬貫

❖ 常用搭配詞

wealthy + n.

　　people, families, individuals, men, merchants, nations, landowners, classes, businessman, parents, country, clients, peasants, women, patrons, friends, groups, households, investors, areas, industrialist, aristocrats, lifestyle, elites.

prosperous (adj.)

❖ 片語

relatively **prosperous**
相當繁榮
Our family business is **prosperous**.
我們的家族事業很興盛。

❖ 常用搭配詞

prosperous + n.

areas, future, years, regions, merchant, city, parts, town, south, farmer, family, community, society, port, business, days, period, place, life, shopkeeper, trade, traders, peasant, nation, people.

affluent (adj.)

❖ 片語

affluent society
富裕的社會
in one's more affluent days
在某人比較寬裕的日子

❖ 常用搭配詞

affluent + n.

society, worker, country, west, people, area, suburb, town, business, country, culture, parents, members, visitors, homes, nations, region, neighborhood, times, days.

opulent (adj.)

❖ 片語

opulent and daring
富有又勇於冒險

opulent and green
富有且沒經驗

opulent elite
富有的菁英

❖ 常用搭配詞

opulent + <u>n.</u>

　surroundings, comfort, bouquet, interior, fabric, villa.

well-off (adj.)

❖ 片語

relatively **well-off**
相當富裕

reasonably **well-off**
還算富裕

moderately **well-off**
中等富裕

❖ 常用搭配詞

well-off + _n._

pensioners, people, farmers, families, men, landlords, homeowners, states.

綜合整理

rich	表示財物眾多，也指資源豐富，後面的名詞可能是人、礦藏、農作物、動物棲息地、地理區域等，意義範圍較廣。
wealthy	強調長時間的富有，後面的名詞以人為主，而且時常是複數。
prosperous	正式用字，表示人富有且成功，也可形容繁榮的社會、地區、或時期。
well-off	well-off後面的名詞以人為主，是rich的委婉說法（表示謙虛）。
affluent	正式用字，表示人富有而能過著奢華高消費的生活，後面的名詞可以是人、地區、或時期。
opulent	正式用字，表示人富有而能過著奢華高消費的生活。後面的名詞可以是人、建築物、環境等。

Unit 92 富麗堂皇、壯觀、雄偉

StringNet語料庫出現次數

magnificent	splendid	glorious	majestic
1959	1573	1072	274

magnificent (adj.)

❖ 片語

a **magnificent** set of rubies

一組燦爛的紅寶石

magnificent views over the sea

海上壯麗的景觀

❖ 常用搭配詞

magnificent + n.

view, setting, scenery, collection, display, building, surroundings, work, palace, spectacle, country, sight, monument, piece, court, hall, beach, animal, library, cathedral, villa, room, castle, bird, mountain, sea, backdrop, tree, waterfall, cliff, carpet, painting.

glorious (adj.)

❖ 片語

a glorious dawn
光輝的黎明
glorious cathedral of Wells
富麗堂皇的威爾斯教堂

❖ 常用搭配詞

glorious + n.

day, views, year, past, sunshine, hair, victory, color, future, summer, morning, moment, success, leader, history, scenery, sense, sunset, display.

splendid (adj.)

❖ 片語

the splendid piece of furniture
華麗的家具
the splendid view across the lake
湖上燦爛的景致

❖ 常用搭配詞

splendid + n.

views, work, time, piece, day, sight, castle, house, place, creature, fish, hotel, display, harbor, church, building, beach, backdrop.

majestic (adj.)

❖ 片語

a **majestic** lake
壯闊的湖

on a **majestic** scale
氣勢磅薄

❖ 常用搭配詞

majestic + n.

hotel, castle, river, sight, eagle, size, peninsula, mountain, lake, garden, facade.

綜合整理

magnificent	後面名詞可以是視野、自然風景（如山水）、建築物、動植物、藝術作品等。
splendid	後面名詞較常是建築物，也可接視野（view, sight等）。
glorious	指光輝燦爛的景色或顏色，後面名詞是視野（scenery, views）或日出日落，另外也也表示光榮的，後面接時間（如day, moment, history等）。
majestic	在語料庫出現次數少，可形容建築物或自然景觀，特別強調不但壯觀雄偉且鉅大。

索引

秀威經典　　　　　　　　　　　　　　　　　　　學語言06　PD0034

英語辭彙不NG
——StringNet教你使用英文同義字

作　　者 / 李路得
責任編輯 / 陳佳怡
圖文排版 / 賴英珍
封面設計 / 楊廣榕

出版策劃 / 秀威經典
發 行 人 / 宋政坤
法律顧問 / 毛國樑　律師
印製發行 / 秀威資訊科技股份有限公司
　　　　　114台北市內湖區瑞光路76巷65號1樓
　　　　　電話：+886-2-2796-3638　傳真：+886-2-2796-1377
　　　　　http://www.showwe.com.tw
劃撥帳號 / 19563868　戶名：秀威資訊科技股份有限公司
　　　　　讀者服務信箱：service@showwe.com.tw
展售門市 / 國家書店（松江門市）
　　　　　104台北市中山區松江路209號1樓
　　　　　電話：+886-2-2518-0207　傳真：+886-2-2518-0778
網路訂購 / 秀威網路書店：http://www.bodbooks.com.tw
　　　　　國家網路書店：http://www.govbooks.com.tw

2015年12月　BOD一版
定價：490元
版權所有　翻印必究
本書如有缺頁、破損或裝訂錯誤，請寄回更換

國家圖書館出版品預行編目

英語辭彙不NG：StringNet教你使用英文同義字 /
李路得著. -- 一版. -- 臺北市：秀威經典,
2015.12
　面；　公分. -- (語言學習類 ; PD0034)
BOD版
ISBN 978-986-92379-7-0(平裝)

1. 英語　2. 同義詞　3. 詞彙

805.124　　　　　　　　　　　104024388

讀 者 回 函 卡

感謝您購買本書，為提升服務品質，請填妥以下資料，將讀者回函卡直接寄回或傳真本公司，收到您的寶貴意見後，我們會收藏記錄及檢討，謝謝！
如您需要了解本公司最新出版書目、購書優惠或企劃活動，歡迎您上網查詢或下載相關資料：http:// www.showwe.com.tw

您購買的書名：＿＿＿＿＿＿＿＿＿＿＿＿＿＿＿＿＿＿＿＿＿＿＿＿＿

出生日期：＿＿＿＿＿年＿＿＿＿＿月＿＿＿＿＿日

學歷：□高中 (含) 以下　　□大專　　□研究所 (含) 以上

職業：□製造業　□金融業　□資訊業　□軍警　□傳播業　□自由業
　　　□服務業　□公務員　□教職　　□學生　□家管　□其它＿＿＿＿

購書地點：□網路書店　□實體書店　□書展　□郵購　□贈閱　□其他

您從何得知本書的消息？

　□網路書店　□實體書店　□網路搜尋　□電子報　□書訊　□雜誌

　□傳播媒體　□親友推薦　□網站推薦　□部落格　□其他＿＿＿＿＿＿

您對本書的評價：（請填代號　1.非常滿意　2.滿意　3.尚可　4.再改進）

　封面設計＿＿＿＿　版面編排＿＿＿＿　內容＿＿＿＿　文／譯筆＿＿＿＿　價格＿＿＿＿

讀完書後您覺得：

　□很有收穫　□有收穫　□收穫不多　□沒收穫

對我們的建議：＿＿＿＿＿＿＿＿＿＿＿＿＿＿＿＿＿＿＿＿＿＿＿＿＿

＿＿＿＿＿＿＿＿＿＿＿＿＿＿＿＿＿＿＿＿＿＿＿＿＿＿＿＿＿＿＿＿＿

＿＿＿＿＿＿＿＿＿＿＿＿＿＿＿＿＿＿＿＿＿＿＿＿＿＿＿＿＿＿＿＿＿

＿＿＿＿＿＿＿＿＿＿＿＿＿＿＿＿＿＿＿＿＿＿＿＿＿＿＿＿＿＿＿＿＿

11466
台北市內湖區瑞光路 76 巷 65 號 1 樓
秀威資訊科技股份有限公司　　　收
BOD 數位出版事業部

....

（請沿線對折寄回，謝謝！）

姓　　名：＿＿＿＿＿＿＿＿＿　年齡：＿＿＿＿＿　性別：□女　□男

郵遞區號：□□□□□

地　　址：＿＿＿＿＿＿＿＿＿＿＿＿＿＿＿＿＿＿＿＿＿＿＿

聯絡電話：(日)＿＿＿＿＿＿＿＿＿＿　(夜)＿＿＿＿＿＿＿＿＿＿

E-mail：＿＿＿＿＿＿＿＿＿＿＿＿＿＿＿＿＿＿＿＿＿＿＿＿